SOMETHING BETTER

Jim Bates

DARK MYTH
www.darkmythproductions.com/publications

Dark Myth Publications, a division of
The JayZoMon/Dark Myth Company.
21050 Little Beaver Rd, Apple Valley, CA 92308

ISBN: 978-1-7372947-2-6

First Printing July 2021

Dark Myth Publications is a registered trademark of The JayZoMon/Dark Myth Company

10 9 8 7 6 5 4 3 2 1

Table of Contents

Table of Contents (Cont'd)

Dedications

Dedicated to my son, Yuri Jeremiah Bates. You've enriched my life in ways I could never have imagined. May your dreams continue to come true.

Introduction

Something Better began in 2019, with me challenging myself to write about the effects of global warming on earth in the year 2220. I thought a series of stories based on four main characters would be a good way to go. In October 2019, I sent the first story, "At the Biodome", to World of Myth Magazine and was thrilled when Stephanie said that she was interested in publishing it. Thirteen more stories followed which are now combined into this novella.

Something Better would not have happened without the opportunity to have submitted the stories to World of Myth Magazine in the first place. Many thanks go out to Stephanie Bardy and David Montoya for your incredible encouragement and support, not only of me, but of so many other writers as well. I'm thrilled to have this novella published by you!

I live in a small town twenty miles west of Minneapolis, Minnesota and have seriously been writing since 2015. My stories and poems have appeared in nearly three-hundred online and print publications. My short story "Aliens" was nominated by The Zodiac Press for the 2021 Pushcart Prize. My collection of short stories *Resilience* was published in February 2021, by Bridge House Publishing. *Periodic Stories*, a collection of thirty-one stories based on the periodic table, was published by Impspired in March 2021. *Short Stuff* a collection of flash fiction and drabbles will be published by Chapeltown books in the summer of 2021. All of my stories can be found on my blog: www.theviewfromlonglake.wordpress.com.

Jim Bates

June, 2021

SOMETHING BETTER

SOMETHING BETTER

Chapter One

At the Biodome

"**DADDY, LOOK,**" Matt pointed, excitedly. "What's that?"

Quinn smiled. It was good to see his five-year-old son so enthusiastic, but then again everyone who entered the Northwoods Biodome exhibit usually was. He read the sign. "It says it's a Norway Pine. It used to be the state tree of Minnesota."

Matt contemplated for a moment, "A long time ago, right?"

"Right. A really long time."

Matt then spied something stuffed and displayed in a diorama and pointed, "It that a bird?"

"It is," Quinn replied, reading the sign. "It's a cardinal. Probably because it's red."

"Pretty."

A voice over the loudspeaker caught their attention. "All those for the morning tour, line up under the sign to your right."

"That's us, son." Quinn took Matt's hand, and they quickly made their way to where the line was forming. If they were late, he'd pay by having a day knocked off his LifeLine. He was twenty-five years old and had already lost one-hundred and seventy- seven days; nearly half a year shortened from his life span. He wanted to see Matt live at least to be twenty, so he'd have to be careful.

They made it to the line in time, slid their Identification cards into the reader and paused for authorization. When it came through, they waited with the fifty or so other visitors for the tour to begin. A tour that would take them through a living replica of what it looked like in the northern region of the United States, nearly two hundred years earlier.

It made Quinn happy to see Matt so excited. So was he. This was their first trip together to the exhibit, a trip mandated for parents and five-year-olds by the Education Committee of the World Order. He was especially looking forward to being in a different environment than the relentlessly gray world they normally lived in. At least in the Biodome the air was clean, and they didn't have to wear oxygen masks like in The City. They could even hear songbirds singing, though the birds were fake, and the songs were digitalized.

"Years ago, the world was like this," he said to Matt as the tour began.

SOMETHING BETTER

"What happened?"

"It's complicated, but in a nutshell, gases like carbon dioxide increased in the atmosphere, the earth's temperature rose, the polar ice caps melted, and the land turned to desert. It happened fast. Only took about fifty years."

Matt looked concerned. "Were you alive then?"

"No. It was before my time. Your ancestors were, though."

"Ancestors?"

Oops. He'd slipped up. With the World Order mandating a maximum life span of forty years and days knocked off for breaking any rule, no one made it to forty. There were no living ancestors.

"Um, I'll tell you about it later," Quinn said and pointed, "Look at that."

The tour, led by an automated robot, was leaving a hardwood forest, and heading toward a pond surrounded by reeds and cattails. Redwing blackbirds were singing in the background. They were robotic replicas, but Quinn didn't have the heart to tell Matt. There'd be time for those kinds of discussions on another day.

After a walk through a replica of a tall grass prairie, the tour ended with the robot thanking everyone. "Have a super day," it said.

The participants dutifully clapped (not wanting to get a day docked from their LifeLine) and prepared to leave. Quinn and Matt put on their oxygen masks and joined the crowd heading for the exit where a transport carrier was waiting to take them to their respective living areas;

Quinn's, a bunker-like apartment complex near the wind energy farm where he worked, Matt's, a dormitory for children.

He was glad he'd had this time with his son. The World Order controlled every moment of their lives, from where people worked, to what time they slept, to when they saw the one child that married couples were allowed to have. They even controlled what was eaten since food was at a premium. In fact, there was talk of the Maximum Age being lowered from forty to thirty-nine. Not enough food, too many people. Life on planet earth was not getting any better.

When they were seated on the transport carrier, Matt said to his dad, politely, "Thank you, Daddy for taking me. I had a really fun time."

Quinn smiled. He loved his son, and he was glad he'd been able to spend time with him. Once a week wasn't often enough. "I had fun, too."

The first stop was the building were children Matt's age were kept. Quinn wanted to hug him but knew the World Order frowned upon signs of affection. After a brief hesitation, he thought, *What the hell, why not?* and grabbed Matt in a big bear hug, knowing the surveillance cameras would catch him and punish him accordingly by taking a day off his LifeLine. Too bad, he thought, holding his son tighter. Matt hugged him back. He felt his son's sweet breath on his neck, and it made him smile. The hug was worth it.

Finally, Matt squirmed away with delight, giggling. "I'll see you next week, Daddy."

"Okay, son. The History Center, right?"

SOMETHING BETTER

"Right."

"See you then. Bye, bye." Quinn waved.

The transport carrier then headed for the concrete building where Quinn and his wife Karen lived. He watched the landscape passing by outside his window, featureless and gray with dust and ash everywhere, relentlessly depressing. His mind drifted back to the exhibit he and Matt had seen. He loved the colors: the green trees and the blue pond. The red cardinal. Not the gray decay he and Karen and their son lived in every day. It'd be a week before he'd see Matt again and he was already looking forward to it. In fact, at that moment he made a fateful decision. When they got together next time, he was going to hold his son again. Tight. No matter what the consequences. LifeLine be damned. It'd be worth it.

JIM BATES

SOMETHING BETTER

Chapter Two

The Test

QUINN AND HIS wife Karen lived on the fifteenth floor of the fifty-story concrete apartment complex they'd called home for the six years of their marriage. As he hung his oxygen mask on the peg by the door and stepped into the living area, Karen turned to him from her desk, a palpable tension in the air. Something was up.

"I just sent my test in."

"How'd it go?"

"Not good." She slammed her hand down hard. "Damn it! I don't know what went wrong. I know this stuff.

Quinn rushed to her side, knelt, and put a supportive

hand on her arm. "Wasn't the subject microbiology? You're good with that. There's probably nothing to worry about."

"Easy for you to say, Mr. Hot-Shot Engineer."

She was right about him being an engineer. He was pretty good with mechanical and electronic devices of all kinds. A hot shot? Debatable.

Nevertheless, Quinn understood what Karen was worried about. Even though she was brilliant in chemistry and biology, if she didn't do well on the test, the company she worked for, Millennium Microbial, had the authority to dock a day off her LifeLine. She'd already lost thirty-four days during the first twenty-five years of her life, and she didn't want to lose anymore.

Quinn worked at the regional wind energy farm. He was short and wiry with penetrating brown eyes, a closely trimmed beard and a shaved head. Karen was a research biologist. She was a tall as her husband and willowy, with intelligent green eyes, wavy red hair, and faint freckles. The year was 2220. The world was in chaos as a result of climate change and ninety-nine-point nine percent of earth's plant and animal population had ceased to exist. The couple was among those tasked with finding ways to one, in Quinn's case, improve energy production and, two, for Karen, find ways to produce more nutritional food. Both energy usage and a worldwide food shortage were reaching the crisis stage, and something had to be done. There was even talk of lowering the mandated age limit from forty years to thirty-nine.

Quinn pulled a chair next to Karen's desk and sat down. As they talked, she could tell her normally low-key husband was unsettled. Finally, she asked, "What up with

SOMETHING BETTER

you?"

"Well, I did something today you need to know about."

"What?" Karen asked, concerned, her test forgotten. "Is it something to do with Matt? Is he okay?"

"No, our son is fine, actually. We had a great time at the Biodome."

She breathed a sigh of relief. "Good."

Before he could tell her more Karen's computer dinged, signifying a message. She looked at Quinn. "Must be the test results. That was fast."

"Fingers crossed."

They watched the monitor as Karen punched a key calling up her message. "It's from them," she said, opening it. Then she smiled, leaped up and shouted, "Yea! I passed. I won't get docked."

She pulled Quinn to his feet, threw her arms around him and they held each other tightly, enjoying the closeness. Their physical attraction for each other helped off-set the dull existence of the world they lived in.

Just then there was another dinging notification. She checked it. "Shit. Finkelstein wants me to come in early." Jerry Finkelstein was her supervisor. "I better go. He's sending the company transport carrier.

"Must be important," Quinn said, poking fun, half joking, half serious.

Quinn and Karen were among a small group of citizens that didn't always play by the rules established by the World Order. They weren't radicals per-se, but they were more free-thinking than most of the population. That attitude sometimes got them into trouble.

"No way. He's just a jerk and likes to show off that he's got enough money to do crap like that."

"I hear you. How about if I walk you down?"

Karen kissed him again. "That'd be nice. Let me grab my oxygen mask. You can finish telling me what you were going to say."

"Oh, it wasn't that big a deal," Quinn said, and grinned, trying to laugh it off. "I'll tell you about it when you get home. For now, let's celebrate you passing that quiz."

Karen was smart, and she knew her husband, but she did have to get to work. She gave him a pointed look. "Okay. But we'll talk when I get home. All right?"

"All right."

After Karen was picked up downstairs to go back to Millennium Microbial, Quinn went back to their apartment. His shift started in an hour, and he had time to go to his computer and check his LifeLine. Yep, that's what he was afraid of. He'd hugged his son when they'd said good-bye which was a big no-no in the far-reaching eyes of the World Order. Showing affection in public was frowned upon. Quinn knew it but didn't care. Hopefully, Karen would understand. They'd docked him two days for his transgression. His life span was getting shorter.

He closed down the computer, went to the sliver of plastic that served as their one window and looked out on the ashen grey landscape of the world he and Karen and Matt lived in. A world he was willing to shorten his life span by a day at a time, if necessary, just to have physical contact with his boy. Something he planned to keep doing.

SOMETHING BETTER

LifeLine be damned. It was the price he'd have to pay. After all, he wasn't going to live forever.

JIM BATES

SOMETHING BETTER

Chapter Three

Millennium Microbial

KAREN SETTLED INTO her seat of the company transport carrier, waved good-bye to Quinn, and opened her company issued computer. Millennium Microbial liked to called it a Data Tablet, but Karen and everyone else called it a laptop because that's what it was.

She turned her attention to her laptop, knowing exactly what was on Finkelstein's mind. He wanted an update on the project she and the other two members of her team had been working on. As she brought up her records, a shudder went through the normally unflappable young project leader. Her team had been studying the possibility of improving the nutritional value of the world's dwindling food supply. They'd been running a series of tests for two months and had the preliminary results and they weren't good. The process they tested was going to be prohibitively costly and no manufacturing company in their right mind would go for it. With that being the case, people would have to make do with more chemically produced nutritional supplements and get used to taking more injections of the body's much needed proteins. It was the only way.

Distressed to have to present such dire results to her boss, Karen closed her computer and looked out upon the lifeless land that was now planet Earth, the end result of two hundred years of global warming. Desolate brown landscapes, non-descript concrete structures to live and work in and a dusty atmosphere making daytime seem like perpetual twilight, all combined to make the outside world endlessly depressing. She sighed and focused her attention on the task ahead and the presentation to her boss, a really depressing thought, even worse than the landscape outside she was traveling through.

The transport carrier parked in the tunnel underneath Millennium Microbial, and Karen exited and made her way to the entrance. Two security guards checked her for banned electronics and a reader scanned her index fingerprint. When the guards acknowledged who she was, she was safe to enter, and they let her in through massive steel security doors.

The inside of the building was a brightly lit and starkly sterile space of whitewashed walls, wide hallways, and gleaming black tile floors. No color anywhere. She took the elevator to the fifth floor and made her way to her cubicle where her co-worker and friend Jen popped her head over the partition.

"Hi, there," Karen greeted her.

"Hi," Jen said. Then she leaned closer and got right to the point, "Did you hear about the meeting? Finkelstein wants all of us, me, you and Randy, to attend." Jen pointed to the empty cubicle where their other team member's workstation was located.

Jen had close-cropped auburn hair and deep-set amber eyes. Her short stature belied the fact that she was a fireball of energy. She was also the fittest person Karen knew. A few years earlier on her way home from work Jen had been attacked by two thugs. Her screams brought a half-interested policeman from the WOSP to the scene who scared them off before things got out of hand, but the horror of the event stayed with her.

"I never want to feel like a victim again," she'd told Karen the next day. "Things are changing right now."

She began working out, primarily lifting weights, and doing aerobic exercises in her small apartment with a passion bordering on obsession and was now in tip-top shape. She was also a loving, caring person, and the same age as Karen. They had worked together for five years. The entire time they'd been employed by the bio-engineer company. Their friendship was the only bright spot at work as far as Karen was concerned.

Karen nodded. "Yeah, I heard about it. He called me in on my day off."

"I know and it sucks. You could use a break," Jen lowered her voice and sympathetically shook her head. There was no love lost from either of them toward their demanding boss. She switched gears and asked, "Do you know what the meeting's about?"

"I'm pretty sure he wants an update on our project."

"So soon? We've only had two months to work on it."

"Yeah, but you know him. He expects miracles and doesn't care about scientific method or process at all. Just results." She grimaced, "What a jerk."

Jen whispered, "Yeah, I know. He's the absolute worst." She was cautious about anyone overhearing their conversation and with good reason. The company was ripe with employees who would do anything to get ahead. It made for more stress in an already stressful work environment.

"No kidding. I'm definitely not looking forward to this." Karen checked the clock on the wall. "Well, you ready? We should get going."

"I'm all set." Jen said and pointed behind her to the empty cubicle. "Randy's in the break room." Of the three of them, he would be considered the quiet one, almost to the point of being withdrawn. He was a brilliant microbiologist, though.

"Let's get him on the way to the meeting. Just let me grab my laptop, it's got my re-cap on it."

Five minutes later the three of them walked in Jerry Finkelstein's office. He took one look at them and checked his ornate watch. With no preliminary greeting, he barked, "Let's get started." He didn't even offer for them to sit down.

Not surprised by his rudeness, Karen, as team leader got right to point, opening her laptop. "I'm assuming you want

SOMETHING BETTER

an update?"

Their boss sat back and smirked. He was a short, squat man with a thin goatee. He looked like a potato, one of the few vegetables that still existed in the world. "Yeah, I do," he challenged her. "Give me your best shot."

Inwardly, Karen grimaced. God, she hated the man. 'Give me your best shot.' Everything was a game to him. In fact, sometimes Karen got the distinct feeling he wanted them to fail, especially her and Jen. He had a bad attitude toward women in general and the two of them in particular and seemed to delight in finding ways of making them prove their worth as competent scientists. This project was one of them.

"Okay," she started her summary, "here's where we're at."

The essence of her presentation was that their research into splitting microbial DNA and trying to genetically engineer a different stain of food was a failure. The plants they developed all died.

But at least they'd learned something, as Karen pointed out in conclusion, "We know what doesn't work. Now we can focus on looking in a different direction."

Finkelstein leapt to his feet and screamed. "I don't want to go in different direction! I wanted this to work and now you're telling me it doesn't. We've already invested a lot of money into this project. What you're telling me is unacceptable." He shook his head as he thrust a finger at Randy. "What about you? You got anything better than this?"

Randy looked sheepishly at Karen. When he did, she felt a sudden clutch in her stomach and knew immediately something bad was going to happen. "Well, to be honest, I do."

Damn, Karen thought to herself. *He's going around us.* She turned to him and yelled, "No, God damn it!"

"Good," Finkelstein said to Randy. "And you," he pointed at Karen. "You shut up." Karen clamped her lips together as he flicked his fingers at her and Jen, like shooing a couple of flies away. "Go away. I want you of here. Both of you. Now!"

They did as they were told but not before Karen and Jen both shot hard stares at Randy on the way out. He avoided their looks of disgust but at least had the decency to blush.

"What was that all about?" Jen whispered once they were outside the office and the door was closed.

"I guess our former teammate is going off on his own. Remember how we talked about trying to genetically engineer a complete DNA helix like they did back in the twenty-first century? I think that's what he's going to talk to Finkelstein about."

"We both know that won't work," Jen said.

"I know. I guess old Randy just wants to try and get on Finkelstein's good side."

Jen coughed out a derisive laugh, "Good luck with that. We both know he doesn't have one."

"Randy doesn't know that I guess. You know, I always thought there was something funny about him."

"Well, you were right." She pointed toward the closed door to emphasize her point. "That's for sure."

The two of them walked back to their cubicles, talking intently. "We could get started on our own research right away, you know," Jen said. "You've got those last findings, right?"

"Yeah, the ones that suggest working with that DNA strand?"

"We can investigate that one protein strand on the fifteenth chromosome."

"Yeah," Karen said, thinking. Then she made her decision. "To hell with Randy and Finkelstein, let's do it. We'll work on it on our own. Let's prove both of them wrong." She set her laptop on her desk and took out her phone, catching Jen's eye. "Give me a second. I'm going to call Quinn. It could be a long night."

Jen replied, almost thinking out loud, "It could be a long few months. If we don't get this worked out..." she let her words trail off.

"Yeah, I know," Karen said. "If we don't come up with a solution to increase the world's food supply..."

"We're dead," Jen said, finishing Karen's thought and cutting her finger across her throat.

"Yeah. Very dead," Karen agreed. They were one of the few select scientists that knew the world's food supply could only last another twenty-five years at most. Then it would be a long and slow death by starvation for the fifteen million people remaining on earth along with the chaos that was sure to accompany it.

The possibility was too horrific to contemplate for long. They had a huge job ahead, but they had confidence in themselves. They looked at each other and solemnly clasped hands in solidarity. *We can do this.*

Then Karen called her husband. "Hey, Quinn, I wanted

you to know I'll be home late. Something's come up at work." She listened and then said, looking at her friend and giving her the universal A-Okay sign, "No, we've got it covered. It' not a problem. Me and Jen can handle it."

SOMETHING BETTER

-

Chapter Four

At the History Center

IT WAS BECOMING more and more apparent to Quinn that he just didn't fit in with the twenty-third century. Especially now in 2220 when he and Matt were growing closer and closer every time they saw each other. More than ever, he wanted to spend more time with his son. It was an emotional connection that began when he'd held Matt in his arms those first few moments after Karen had given birth and before the nurse had whisked him away to be raised in the first of many regional dormitories, with parental time limited to only once a week for four hours.

He'd always remember being told he shouldn't have those feelings. "Too bad buddy," one of the nurses in charge had said back then, smirking unsympathetically as he prepared to take the newborn baby away. "That's just the way it is."

All things considered Quinn thought he'd done a pretty good job of not punching the jerk in the nose right then and there. But that would have caused a scene, something frowned upon by the World Order, so he'd kept his mouth shut, hands in his pockets and his feelings to himself.

However, he did have feelings, strong parental feelings, and in those first few moments after Matt had been born Quinn felt a bond forming between the two of them. He knew Matt had felt it too by the way the little fellow smiled a big, toothless grin whenever Quinn held him. But that was too bad, like the nurse had said, because according to the World Order it wasn't supposed to be like that. Feelings were frowned upon in the twenty-third century. He tried to ignore them, but as Matt got older and Quinn spent more time with him, he realized he had to do something. So, for most of the past year he mulled it over, thinking about what to do, but so far, he'd come up with no plan. Nothing. He was in a quandary.

Then, out of the blue that very morning, while waiting for the transport carrier to drop Matt and about seventy other five-year old's off for a World Order mandated field trip to the regional History Center, the answer had come to him. It was a simple solution, really, elegant to his analytical mind, and the more he thought about it, the more he thought, *'Yes, this is the right thing to do'*. He'd simply steal Matt away from the dormitory where he lived. In short, he'd kidnap his son.

Quinn went over his plan in his mind as he waited for Matt. It took only a moment because the truth of the matter was that he didn't have a plan. Not really. In fact, he hadn't even told Karen about it and realized there'd be hell to pay when he did, but he'd have to deal with that later. For now, he'd do what his heart was telling him and take his son away from the cold, heartless dormitory world that was euphemistically referred to as The Neighborhood by those in charge and start living a different life. A better life. One with he and Karen and Matt together as much as they wanted and not prescribed by the World Order. They'd be a real family, just like he'd seen in documentaries occasionally shown by the World Order, describing how bad things used to be. Well, to Quinn and Karen, things in the *olden days* weren't bad at all. Rather, something to aspire to. Especially when it came to family.

So even though he may not know what exactly he was going to do or how he was going to do it, it felt right, and that was the important thing. After all, he told himself, he wasn't going to live forever.

When Matt stepped from the transport carrier, Quinn took off his oxygen mask and rose from his bench in the waiting area to greet him. Matt was easy to pick out from the other five-year olds because of his bright red hair that was the same shade as his mother's. Even though he was short in stature, the red hair was a dead giveaway, part of a genetic strain that ran through Karen's family and similar to the hair color of her long-departed mother.

Quinn waved to get Matt's attention, who, as soon as he saw his dad, grinned, and waved back. They hurried to each other and instead of the World Order mandated formal handshake, Quinn gave Matt a big hug, ignoring the gasps from the other parents gathered to meet their own children. Quinn didn't care. It felt good to hug his boy, so he did it again. So, what if he lost two more days off his Lifeline, one for each hug? He didn't care. Besides, how could he ignore the wonderful feeling he got when Matt hugged him back. *Take that, World Order Security Police,* he thought to himself. *Too bad if you don't like it.*

Quinn took Matt's oxygen mask and put it along with his own into his backpack. Once they passed through security, they came to the first exhibit. Matt excitedly pointed and read the sign, haltingly, wanting to show off for his dad.

Quinn smiled as Matt turned serious and intoned, "House. Victorian Era. 1900's."

"That's really good, son," Quinn said, complimenting him, appreciating how much better life felt when the two of them were together.

Matt's proud smile quickly faded. "Thank you," he said, politely. "But, Dad, I don't know what it means."

Quinn took Matt's hand, ignoring that it was another violation, and worked his way through the crowd to a nearby bench where they sat down. "That's okay. I'll tell you what I know." In the back of his mind, he saw another day being lopped of his Lifeline.

"Long, long ago, people actually lived in houses like this."

Matt's eye went wide, thinking about the cold, gray concrete structure he lived in. "No way! They did? What happened?"

"Well, you needed wood to make houses like this one and as the world got warmer most of the trees died."

"Trees?"

SOMETHING BETTER

"Yes, like we saw last week in the Biodome."

Matt's eyes lit up. "Oh, yeah! I liked it there."

"Me, too. But remember that the exhibit at the Biodome is like this one. Things aren't like that anymore."

"I know." Matt was quiet for a minute, thinking. Then he said, out of the blue, changing the subject, "Dad, I have to tell you something."

"Sure. What is it?"

"I don't like where I live."

"You mean at The Neighborhood? The dormitory?"

"Yes," he snuffled, tears beginning to form as he tried to be brave.

Quinn's heart went out to him. He put his arm around Matt's thin shoulder and pulled him close. "What is it, Matt? What's the matter, son? You can tell me."

Matt looked up with plaintive eyes and Quinn's heart almost broke, "They're mean to me there, Dad. Plus, I get lonely, and I miss you. And Mom."

The World Order mandated that children be raised according to their strict guidelines. Married couples could have one child and that child was removed from them shortly after birth and raised in a dormitory along with other children of their age. Their indoctrination into World Order philosophy beginning in the cradle. They only saw each other on approved outings, like the one they were on now. For caring parents, like Quinn and Karen, it wasn't much or nearly enough.

Most couples accepted the situation with equanimity, but Quinn and his wife Karen did not. Karen loved Matt deeply but her job as a biochemist for Millennium Microbial forced her to work long hours. Quinn happily picked up the slack. He saw Matt as often as he could, sometimes even taking a day off from his job to go on World Order mandated field trips, like the one they were on today. Any excuse to be with Matt was fine with him; in fact, the more times the better, as far as he was concerned.

Matt's plight touched his father, furthering his resolve to make a drastic change. Quinn took his son's hand and they walked to the next exhibit, a replica of a huge white domed building.

When they stopped in front of it, Matt dutifully read the sign, "The White House. This is where presidents lived. Right up until the World Order took over in 2120."

Matt looked at his dad, confused. "Presidents? I don't get it."

Quinn said, "Way back then, where we're living now, there was a country called the United States of America. When the world temperature started getting warmer and the crops began failing and the oceans started rising, all..." he was going to say "All hell broke loose" but he didn't. Instead, he said, "Well, things began changing. Fast. And not for the best." *You can say that again,* he thought to himself.

And things had gotten lots worse since then, too, especially concerning the world's food supply. Or lack of it. The project Karen was currently working on was investigating ways to improve food production to help increase the dwindling supplies. As she had told Quinn just last night, "The prospects are grim, believe me, but Jen and I are doing our best."

SOMETHING BETTER

And Quinn certainly hoped for the best, but his wife and her team of one had a huge task ahead of them.

Quinn and Matt toured a few other exhibits and Quinn began to notice how subdued the young boy was. It was breaking his heart. He saw Matt for at the most four hours a week and it clearly wasn't enough; for either of them. The time was right to make his move.

As they walked with the group of parents and five-year olds to the cafeteria for lunch, Quinn leaned down and asked, "Matt, let me ask you something."

"What, Dad?" Matt took Quinn's hand.

"How would you like to live with me and your mom?"

Matt's eyes went wide. "Really? Live with you and Mom?"

"Yes. Shhh," Quinn held his finger to his lips. "Not so loud," but he grinned to show he wasn't mad. Suddenly, his heart was pounding. The last thing he needed was to get caught before he'd had a chance to even try to get Matt out of the dormitory. He looked around to make sure no one close by was paying attention. Then he asked, "Would you like that?" He didn't notice a security guard eyeing them suspiciously.

"Live with you and Mom? Oh, yes! Yes, I would."

"I'd like that, too," Quinn said, and smiled as he tousled Matt's thick red hair, accepting that it would result in another deduction from his Lifeline. He didn't care. After today, it really wouldn't matter.

Changing the subject, Quinn asked, "Are you hungry?"

"Yeah. Starving."

They followed the crowd into the cafeteria and the security guard lost interest in them.

"All right, let's get our lunch," Quinn said.

"Goody," said Matt.

But they never did.

Matt's absence wasn't reported until later that evening when he turned up missing at evening bed check. The room he shared with three other boys was quickly searched and then the entire dormitory. Nothing. Matt was nowhere to be found. It was late that night when authorities placed a call to Quinn and Karen at home in their fifty-story concrete apartment complex to tell them the bad news.

Karen answered, "Hello?" She listened for a minute and then shouted, "Matt's missing?" Her voice rose in anger. "Well, you'd better find him! Fast!! Because if you don't, I'll..." After yelling in the phone for five minutes, she angrily hung up. Then she smiled to herself. *There, that should convince them I don't know anything about what happened*.

Then she dialed Quinn. They'd been in constant contact since Quinn had discovered the vacant building six hours earlier and had called Karen. They were now talking every hour or so, keeping each other updated on what was going on.

He picked up. "Karen?"

"Yeah. The security police just called about Matt being missing. I blew up at them. When I was done screaming, I'm pretty sure they didn't think either you or I had anything to do with it."

SOMETHING BETTER

"You did good, honey." Quinn breathed a sigh of relief that Karen could hear over the phone.

"So," she asked, "how are you two doing?"

Quinn pulled Matt to him and kissed the top of his head. They were sitting in the third and top floor of an abandoned building on the outskirts of the city, five miles from the History Center and a couple of miles from the apartment building where they lived. The building was filthy, and they were cold and hungry but that didn't matter because they were together. "Good. I found some old blankets. I've got some food I stole from the cafeteria. We're going to have something to eat later."

Karen checked the time. It was nearly midnight. Quinn and Matt had been on the run for nearly twelve hours. She was mad at her husband in one respect for taking Matt without telling her, but she was also proud of him for sticking up for Matt and doing what he thought was best for him. "I'll get some food and water and bring you some other supplies tomorrow morning. Early. How's that sound?"

"Sounds good. Perfect." Then he asked, "Do you want to say hi to Matt?"

Karen's eyes welled up in tears of joy, "Yes! Of course, I do."

Matt came on the phone, "Hi, Mom. Dad and I are having an adventure."

Karen smiled. "That's good, honey." She could imagine Quinn telling Matt something like that, something to make them be fugitives seem a lot less serious than it was. But it was serious. They were wanted by the WOSP, the brutal law enforcement agency of the World Order. Quinn would certainly be imprisoned if he were caught, maybe even put to death, and she couldn't let that happen. She'd do whatever she could to keep her husband and son safe, starting with bringing them much needed supplies tomorrow.

After a few minutes Karen said, "Okay, I should get going. I love you, Matt."

"I love you, too, Mom."

"Now, please let me talk to your dad."

"All right." Matt handed the phone over.

"Hi," Quinn said, trying to sound upbeat.

Karen wasn't having any of it. "My god, Quinn, what were you thinking? More to the point, what *are* you thinking? Do you know how dangerous this is? The WOSP aren't going to be messing around. They'll want to make an example out of you and I'm worried about what they'll do if they find you."

Matt snuggled next to his dad; a feeling Quinn wouldn't trade for anything. "Yeah, I know, Karen. But I'm glad I did it." He had explained to her earlier what Matt had been telling him about dorm life and how some of the kids were being physically mistreated by some of the staff. To make matters worse, the more he and Matt talked the more Quinn was able to read between the lines and figure out that some of the poor children were also being sexually assaulted as well. "I just felt it was the right thing to do; to rescue Matt from that place and make sure he was safe."

Karen was quiet for a moment and then told him, "I know. I'm just worried. I'm sorry for getting mad. I love you more than ever for doing that. You did the right thing." She paused before continuing, her voice full of resolve, "Look, let's make this work. Like I said, I'll bring you food and water on my way to work. Okay?" Quinn listened, hearing the determination in her voice. Once Karen made up her mind anything was possible. It was good to have her on his side.

"Yes, absolutely! Look, I'm sorry. I know I should have thought this through better, but…"

"Cool it, Quinn," she interrupted him. "What's done is done. I love you and I love Matt. We'll figure this out."

They talked some more, arranging where to meet and other logistics, both of them aware that their lives had now changed forever. After Karen hung up, she held her phone in her hand and stared at the blank screen. She had one final thought: Quinn could never come home again. He was a fugitive, and it was up to her to help keep him safe. He and their son. Could she do it?

Karen spent the next few hours getting supplies together before she came up with her answer. And the answer was this: Yes. Yes, she would do what she could to keep her family safe because, liked she'd said on the phone, she loved Quinn and she loved Matt. Somehow, she'd figure out a way to make it work.

When she had all the supplies together, Karen lay down to rest but couldn't sleep. A dingy, grey twilight crept across the sky outside the one narrow window in the apartment. After a few minutes, she sighed and got up. Tomorrow was already here. It was going to be a long day. She hoped she was ready for it.

JIM BATES

SOMETHING BETTER

Chapter Five

The Hideout

KAREN CHECKED HER backpack before leaving the apartment, going through her mental checklist to make sure she had the essentials: water, food, and clothes. Then she added the most critical item, a box of air filters, one each for Quinn and Matt's oxygen masks. The carbon dioxide level in the earth's troposphere was so high that a person would suffocate in minutes without the purifying power of the air filter pads. Place them into the air chamber of the mask and you were good to go. At least for a few days. Then they'd become clogged with impurities and had to be replaced.

Speaking of...Karen put a new filter in her mask, shouldered the pack and left the apartment. She took the elevator down fifteen stories to the ground level and exited, slipping on her oxygen mask as she went outside. Instead of boarding a transport carrier to take her to work, she took a left and headed out on her own, walking through The City and its foul air. The earth's atmosphere was so thick with dust and other air born particulates that the sky was perpetually light brown. No one ever saw the sun, or clouds, for that matter. After the buildup to global warming nearly two hundred years earlier and with the subsequent dying off of so many plants, animal and insect species, the earth's temperature had stabilized at sixty-eight degrees which was about ten degrees warmer than it had been.

Karen didn't have time to think about any of that. She had about two miles to go to get to where Quinn and Matt were waiting in their hideout. This early, the streets were nearly deserted, and she had little trouble avoiding the few pedestrians she encountered. Most people preferred to travel by transport carrier or not travel at all, choosing instead to be in the controlled environment of their apartment or place of employment. Her plan was to drop off the supplies with Quinn and Matt and then board a carrier and go to work.

As she hurried through The City's bleak streets, she was conscious of the security cameras mounted nearly every one-hundred feet or so on the sides of buildings. She avoided looking directly at them, knowing that their recognition software could be used to identify her. Or maybe not. She knew that many of the cameras were inoperable and hadn't worked right for years. They were only used as a ploy by the WOSP to keep citizens in line. Well, she'd just have to chance it that the ones she was passing weren't watching her. She hurried on, eager to see

SOMETHING BETTER

her husband and son.

Quinn and Matt been hiding out for nearly twenty-four hours and were waiting hungerly for Karen, hunger being the operative word. They had spent a restless night huddled together on the cement floor of the building they were hiding in, not really sleeping but resting fitfully.

They'd gotten up for good early that morning cold and hungry. The food Quinn had stolen from the history center's cafeteria they'd eaten the night before and it hadn't been nearly enough to quell their ravenous appetites.

"Dad, I'm hungry," Matt complained, rubbing his stomach. "I'm really hungry."

Quinn pulled his son to him and held him tight, rocking him gently. "I know. Just hang in there. Mom will be here with food, soon. Just try to hold on a little longer, okay?"

"Okay," Matt's tiny voice squeaked because his throat was so dry. They needed water, too.

Quinn took off his jacket and wrapped Matt in it. "Just lie here for a minute. I'm going to check outside.

Cautiously he went to the window and peered out. There was nothing to see but The City with its brown sky, grey buildings, and a nearly empty street. He checked his phone for any messages from Karen but there were none. The time indicated on it was 6 am. Karen would have left the apartment by now and was probably on her way. He was sure of it. She should be able to cover the two miles to get to them in about half an hour.

"Mom will be here shortly," Quinn said, going back to Matt and sitting on the floor next to him. He had an idea.

35

"Here, let's play that game I showed you last night." He took a small, rounded piece of metal out of his pocket and held it in his hand. "Okay, here's the prize." Then he put both of his hands behind his back. "Now..." he said, lowering voice and making it sound mysterious,"...which hand holds the magic coin?"

Matt giggled. He was thrilled beyond his wildest dreams to be playing with his father. At the dormitory, no one ever played with him because children weren't allowed to play with each other. Interactions were discouraged upon threat of punishment. Children were required to attend classes that indoctrinated them into the ways being good citizens for the World Order. Any free time they had was spent watching instructional and educational videos. Playing together? Never. For Matt, playing a game with his dad was the most fun he'd ever had in his entire young life.

Matt giggled some more and pointed, "That one, Dad."

Quinn made a quick adjustment and then pulled out the hand Matt had guessed. He kept it closed and said, his voice still sounding mysterious, "Let's see. Let's see. Is it? Is this it?" Then he quickly opened his hand displaying the small piece of metal, the magic coin. "Yes, it is!" he exclaimed. "You're the winner!"

"Yea!" Matt cheered as he took the metal into his tiny hand, the little prize which meant more to him than one could ever imagine. Then he threw his arms around his father's neck and hugged him. "Oh, Dad, this is so much fun."

Quinn smiled the biggest smile he'd ever had in his life as he held his son tight. The time they'd spent together since yesterday when he'd kidnapped Matt had been just the way he'd always imagined it'd be. It felt so good, so right. He'd made the right decision. He knew it. No matter what the consequences of his actions against the World Order, this last day together with Matt had been more than worth it. And he wanted more.

"Yes, it is fun, Matt. It really is."

Karen turned the corner of the street where the hideout was located and took out her phone. She sent Quinn a quick message. *I'm here. Just down the block.*

Quinn's phone beeped and he checked. Reading Karen's message, a smile appeared. He said to Matt, "Good news. Your mom's here."

"Goody!"

Quinn smiled. During their time together during the past day, he'd never seen his son so happy. He sent a reply message. *Come on down the block. We'll meet you at street level, at the doorway.* Then to Matt he said, "Let's go see your mom."

"Okay!" Matt ran across the concrete floor, dust lifting from his little footsteps. At the doorway leading from the room, he turned and motioned with his arm, keeping his voice down like Quinn had taught him, "Come on Dad."

Quinn hurriedly joined Matt where the stairs lead down to the street. He took Matt's hand and was about to start descending the steps when he stopped suddenly and listened. He heard voices. *What was going on?*

"Matt," he whispered, "stand still and don't move,"

Matt obeyed immediately and turned to his father; a

questioning look on his face. "What?" he whispered.

Quinn pulled him close and whispered, "I don't know."

He moved as close as he dared to the top of the stairs and listened carefully. He could hear Karen's voice. And someone else's.

Down on the sidewalk, next to the entryway to the building, Karen had been stopped by a big man dressed in dark blue overalls, the uniform of a World Order Security Police.

She quickly collected herself. "Look, buddy," she said, trying to keep the nervousness out of her voice. "Just leave me alone. I'm not doing anything wrong."

The man was wearing a specialized helmet with a clear face guard. Around his huge stomach he wore a belt filled with canisters and weapons. He was eyeing Karen suspiciously.

"We'll see about that. What's in your backpack?"

"Nothing," Karen said. Their voices carried up the stairwell and Quinn could hear a slight tremor in her voice. She was frightened, but he bet she was doing a good job keeping her fear hidden. That's the way she was, confidently assertive without being overly aggressive. "Just some things I'm bringing to the donation center."

Quinn smiled at his wife's quick thinking. The donation center accepted used goods that were then distributed throughout the region. It was one of the few opportunities for citizens to actually add a day to their lifeline, instead of having one removed.

SOMETHING BETTER

"Really," the officer said, skeptically. "Let's have a look."

Nothing was said for a few minutes while Karen's backpack was being searched. Next to Quinn, Matt became restless. "Dad..."

"Hush," Quinn put his fingers to his lips. "Mom will be here soon. Let's just listen. It's a game to see how long we can be quiet."

"Okay, Dad." Matt agreed and grinned, mimicking zipping his lips shut, prompting Quinn to smile. *Where'd he learn to do that?*

Voices from down below interrupted his thoughts. It was the security guard's loud, authoritative voice, "Okay. This looks fine. I'll let you be on your way, little lady. Just be careful around here. There are criminals all over the place."

"I will. Thanks," Karen said, her relief palatable.

Quinn hurried to the window where he could see Karen hurrying down the street and around the corner. In a few minutes he received a message. *Is the coast clear?*

He sent a message back, *'Yes. Hurry on back. We'll meet you'.*

Five minutes later he and Matt met Karen at the street level entrance and quickly led her up the stairs to the third floor.

When Karen entered the space, she looked around and said, joking in spite of the gravity of the situation, "Home sweet home. I love what you've done with the place."

Quinn smiled. As serious as his wife normally was, she really did have a good sense of humor, and he appreciated that she now used it to help make things less intense for

Matt. They kissed briefly but were interrupted by their son who ran to his mom and grabbed her around the waist, "Oh, Mom, it's so good to see you."

Karen knelt on the floor and hugged him tightly, tears in her eyes. "Oh, Matt, I love you so much."

"I love you, too, Mom."

Quinn let Karen and Matt have their reunion together and began to empty the pack. He set out the food, water and the clothes and the other supplies.

Then he looked at Karen as she still held onto Matt, "That was close down there."

"Yeah, it was. We were all lucky."

"We're safe now," Quinn commented, going to them, and wrapping his arms around the two people he loved most in the world.

After a minute, Karen said, laughing, "Okay enough of the hugging. Let me get you both something to eat. You must be starved."

Matt grinned, "Well, I guess I am."

She gave Matt a protein bar and kissed his forehead. "Sweetheart, can you wait right here a minute?" She looked at Quinn pointedly, "Your dad and I need to talk."

"Sure, Mom." He started eating his bar and asked between bites, "Mom, this is really good. Can I have another one."

Karen smiled and handed him one. "Sure."

Then she led Quinn over to the far side of the room and said, "We're all in trouble."

SOMETHING BETTER

Quinn felt the bottom drop out of his stomach. "Why, what's up?"

"You know that WOSP guy? The guy who stopped me?"

"Yeah. I overheard everything. You did great."

"Well, you didn't overhear it all. Before he let me go, he got kind of weird. He looked around all mysterious and I knew right away something was up. Then he asked me if I'd seen someone. I asked, 'Who?' He opened one of the cases on his belt and took out phone. He showed me the image on it. 'This guy,' he said. I almost fainted."

Quinn felt beads of sweat break out on his brow. This wasn't going to be good news. "Who was it?" he asked, knowing he really didn't have to. He knew the answer.

Karen took a deep breath and let it out. "Quinn, it was a picture of you. A recent one they got a hold of somehow. Bald head. Trimmed beard. And he had one of Matt, too. You could see his red hair perfectly." She looked her husband in the eye. "We've got trouble, buddy. Big trouble. They're looking for us."

Out of all the thoughts that just went shooting through Quinn's brain, one had stood out. And it wasn't a thought so much as a statement. Karen has said, 'Us.'

"Us?" He asked. What do you mean by that? They should just be looking for me and Matt. Not you."

"Yeah, well, not anymore."

"What do mean?"

"Karen took a step forward and hugged him. "Here's the deal. We've been married six years. We have a five-year-old son. We're a family and families stay together. Right?" She paused and leaned back and looked him in the eyes. "I made a decision on the way over here. I'm going to be staying with you."

"What?" Quinn was incredulous.

"Yeah, that's what families do. Right? They stick together and I'm staying with you."

Quinn was almost speechless but not quite, "What about the WOSP?"

"Too bad about them. Me and you are smart. We'll figure out a way."

Just then Matt came over and asked, "Mom do you want something to eat?"

Karen hugged her son. "Sure." She looked over his head at Quinn who was looking pensive. "Don't worry. I'm working on a plan. We'll figure it out." Then she took her husband and son in each of her hands and said, "Let's all get something to eat. We'll do something like they used to do in the old days. It was called a picnic." She winked at Quinn and then looked at Matt and said, "It'll be fun."

"Oh, goody," he said, as the three of them sat down together.

Quinn decided to put his worries aside. Like Karen had just said, they were a family and families stuck together and that's what they were going to do. They had time later to figure out what to do. Plus, Karen had said she was working on a plan, and when Karen got going on an idea it was always a good thing. They'd talk later. For now, they were going to be a family, and they were going to have a picnic.

So, they did. They had a picnic and none of could

remember ever having had such a wonderful meal. Or a better time.

JIM BATES

SOMETHING BETTER

-

Chapter Six

Preparations

"**WHERE THE HELL** is she?" Jerry Finkelstein thundered.

"Karen just called and said she was on her way," Jen told her boss that morning as she looked him in the eye and didn't cower beneath his wrath. "Don't worry about it. She said she'd forgotten a flash drive at home. She was working on an idea for the project all last night."

Finkelstein seemed somewhat placated. "Well, that's good then. You both need to step it up if we're going to get more funding."

"Yes, sir," Jen said, as Finkelstein stalked away from her cubicle, missing the sarcasm in her voice. Then he turned and pointed a threatening finger, "I want a report emailed to me by the beginning of next week. Today's Wednesday, so you'd better hurry up."

"Yes, sir. We will, sir," Jen said, fighting the urge to salute, but he didn't hear. Finkelstein was already storming away. *Man*, Jen thought to herself, *what a jerk*.

For the next hour she worked on her computer. Jen had lied to Finkelstein. She had no idea where Karen was and was getting worried. She knew Karen had a lot on her mind with her husband and son, but it was unlike her to not stay in touch at work.

Just then a familiar face poked around the corner of her cubicle and whispered, "Hi, there."

Jen looked up. "Karen," she exclaimed, but her immediate happiness at seeing her friend was replaced by one of immediate concern. Karen's normally calm and controlled demeanor was haggard, and sleep deprived. "Oh, my god. Karen what's going on? Where have you been?"

Karen put a finger to her lips and kept her voice low, "Come with me. I'm not sure how much time I've got."

When Jen gave her a questioning look, Karen grabbed her by the arm and said, "Come on. I've got something to tell you."

They hurried out of the cubicle area and down a long hallway to the elevator bank where they went up five floors to the employee break room. They each got a cup of tea from a vending machine and went to a table alongside the wall, well out of the way of the dozen or so other employees scattered about.

When they were settled, Jen gave Karen a questioning

look. "What gives? You look awful. Is something the matter with Quinn?"

Karen took a nervous sip, leaned forward, and said, "Promise you won't tell anyone?"

"I promise."

Karen took a deep breath, "Well, you're right. It has to do with Quinn, but there's a lot more to it." She quickly filled Jen in about how Quinn had grown tired of seeing Matt for only a few hours a week during World Order approved visits. "Yesterday he did something crazy. While they were on a field trip to the History Center, he kidnapped Matt. They eventually found a hideout in an abandoned office building near the outskirts of The City.

"It's only a few miles from our apartment building. I went there this morning and brought them supplies."

Jen leaned close, "My god, that's incredible. What are you going to do?" She wanted desperately to give her friend a supportive hug, but the World Order's surveillance cameras were everywhere and the two of them didn't need any more trouble than Karen was already in.

"I'm going to go with them," Karen said. "I made the decision this morning. They're my family and it would kill me not to ever see them again."

"What? Do you realize what that means?" The ramifications flew through Jen's mind and none of them good. Karen had essentially signed her death warrant. The WOSP would eventually find them and when they did if they didn't kill them right away, they'd use Karen and Quinn to make a point: Don't Go Against the World Order. Then they'd be executed for being a danger to society and that would be that.

"You know what'll happen if you get caught," Jen said, her voice shaking. "I'm so frightened for you,"

"Look," Karen tried to explain herself, "The World Order only lets us live to be forty years old anyway. They try to keep us in line by threatening to take days off our precious lifeline for any stupid infraction they can think of. I lost a day by running across the street against a red light when there wasn't a vehicle even in sight. Quinn's lost nearly two-hundred days."

In spite of the seriousness of the situation, Jen smiled, "Well, he is a bit of a rebel."

Karen couldn't help but agree. "Yeah, I know." She took a sip of tea and said, "Here's the deal. Quinn and I have been married for six years and we're really happy with each other. We love Matt but the problem is that he's raised away from us at the stupid concrete dormitory the World Order calls The Neighborhood. One or the other of us can only see Matt once a week for four hours. The rest of the time the poor kid is being indoctrinated to the ways of the World Order."

"I know. It sucks."

"No kidding. Most parents don't mind, but we do. The longer we're together as a family, the more we feel that being parents to Matt is the most important way to spend our time. I mean were twenty-five years old and aren't even going to make it to forty. In the end, seeing Matt for only four hours a week wasn't cutting it for Quinn. Me neither when it came right down to it."

"So, what are you going to do?"

SOMETHING BETTER

Karen sadly shook her head. "Jen, I have to be honest. Even though I'm going with them, I haven't figured out a plan yet. I just don't know how we're going to pull it off."

Jen was shocked. Normally Karen never made a move without thinking through all the details and possible consequences.

"You can't stay where you are now, right? In that abandoned building? The WOSP will eventually find you."

"I know." Karen checked the time on her phone. "It's been about twenty-four hours since Quinn took Matt. The dorm called me last night and reported him missing. I got mad! Yelled, and blamed them for Matt's disappearance."

Jen grinned, "Good move."

Karen nodded and agreed, "Yeah, I thought so. I know they called the WOSP because I bumped into one of them this morning out on the street when I was bringing some supplies to Quinn and Matt. He showed me a recent photo of both of them."

"Oh no! That's not good."

"Right. I feel like the noose is tightening and the guys haven't even been on the run for a day yet."

"On top of that, Finkelstein wants a report from us on Monday."

"What! Why? I thought he didn't want anything to do with us when he gave the project to our former team member." Karen used finger quotes around 'team member' to show her distain for Randy for stabbing Karen and Jen in the back and taking credit for their project.

"Who knows. Maybe Finkelstein realized that he made a

mistake by listening to Randy and giving the project to him."

Karen laughed derisively, "It's only been a day." Then she thought for a minute and said, "You know, our idea is a good one."

"I know. Looking at that special gene and seeing if we could splice it's DNA with..."

Karen put her finger to her lips, "Shh. You never know who's listening," but she smiled as she said it. If someone were listening, they'd be done for anyway. Nevertheless, it felt good to be talking to Jen. She loved her friendship with the woman she'd been working with for the last five years and was going to miss her.

Karen changed the subject, "Here's my idea for our project." She took out her laptop and started it up and showed the file to Jen. "This is a good start, and you can use this as a beginning. You can flesh it out and show it to Finkelstein next Monday. I'll be long gone by then." She paused and didn't have to elaborate because the near future was obvious. Today was Thursday. Next Monday she would either be dead or free. Then she shook the thought from her mind and continued, "He should like it. Maybe even give you a raise."

Jen took a chance and patted the back of Karen's hand. "Don't worry. I'll be fine." Then she switched gears. "Getting back to your predicament. I've been thinking, and I think I have an idea."

"Really?" Karen leaned forward, intrigued, "What? Tell me."

And Jen did. When she was finished, Karen grinned and

said, "Oh, wow! That's a great plan."

"I'm glad you like it," Jen smiled. "And I haven't even told you the best part."

"What's that?"

"I'm coming with you."

"What?"

"Yeah, I've had it with this place. Plus, I can help you take care of Matt."

"You know how dangerous this whole thing is?"

"Not really, but sort of I do." She took a nervous breath and let it out and flexed her muscle, showing her weight-lifters bulge. "But no matter what, though, you might need some muscle."

In spite of the seriousness of the moment, they both laughed.

"You're sure?" Karen asked.

Jen leveled her gaze and said, "I'm sure. Honest. You're my best friend. My only friend. I want to go with you."

Karen could see that Jen was serious. "Okay," she said. "If you're sure."

"Yeah, I'm sure."

"Okay. You're on board." Karen patted her on the hand and then shifted gears, "Okay, then, let's get busy. I want to cover our tracks here and try to buy some time. First off, lets outline that report."

It was around 6:00 pm that evening when Karen returned to the hideout. She had Jen with her and quickly explained to

Quinn that she was going to join them. "Glad you have you with us," Quinn said, greeting them both and hugging Karen. Then he pointed and asked, "What's this?"

They had stopped at both of their apartments on the way to pick up the necessary supplies they'd need to move on to the next phase to the plan.

Karen gave Matt and hug and then set down her backpack and took out a couple of bottles.

Quinn looked perplexed. "What's all this?"

Karen smiled and pointed to Jen. "Tell him. It's your plan."

"I brought some bottles of dye. We can dye our hair to help change our appearance."

"I brought some other clothes, too," Karen added. "Hopefully, we can get ourselves looking different so when we're out on the street no one from the WOSP will recognize us." Quinn grinned at Karen, "Sounds like you've been busy."

"We have. We'll leave tonight. Jen reminded me of the Regional Food Storage Facility on the edge of The City. It's only five miles from here and buses go there all the time. We'll change our appearance and take a bus out there. Once we get off the bus, we can cut across country to get beyond the city limits. No one ever goes out there. Once we're out in the country, we'll be safe."

In Quinn's mind the hazards popped up like a bad dream, the main one getting caught by the WOSP. They'd definitely be looking for them now and if they were caught, they'd certainly be killed. But if they were careful and used their brains, they could make it.

SOMETHING BETTER

"It's a long way to go for Matt," Quinn said crouching down and hugging his son. He looked the young boy in the eye. "Are you up for it?"

"I am, Dad," Matt said. "It'll be an adventure."

Karen looked at her little family, which now included Jen and said, "Yes, it certainly will be."

A few hours later Karen and Jen's hair was dyed black, Quinn's beard was shaved off and he and Matt were wearing a long hair wigs that Jen had brought from her apartment. Jen pointed to Matt, "He looks like a girl, now. Just in case they're looking for a small boy, this will throw them off. Hopefully." She looked at Quinn and shrugged her shoulders, making a joke, "You, well, don't expect to get asked out on a date."

In spite of himself, Quinn laughed. "Don't worry."

Ever serious, Karen ignored them. "Okay, then, we're ready," she said. She looked at Jen. "You still sure about joining us?"

"I am."

Matt had taken a shine to the young woman. "I'm glad she's coming. I like her."

Quinn looked at Karen. "All set?"

In Karen's mind flashed a scenario where Quinn had not kidnapped their son and none of this had happened. Life would have gone on the way it had been going; all the way up to their mandatory death by the World Order. Compared to what they were doing now, to be honest, it was not much of a life. At least now she felt alive. Now their family was all together. Now all they had to do was to evade the WOSP and get out of the city and into the country to safety.

Karen hugged Quinn and gave him a quick kiss. "Time's a wasting. Let's get going."

SOMETHING BETTER

-

Chapter Seven

Fugitives

WHEN SHIELD NUMBER 3456 returned from his shift that night, the regional office was in an uproar. All of the shields were called into a meeting with the main man in charge, Commander Basil Langer.

"In no uncertain terms," Langer intoned, "this kidnapper, or, possibly kidnappers, must be brought to justice. The fugitive took his son from the safety of The Neighborhood, and we now have reason to believe his wife and one other person have joined him. We are mobilizing in full force at 0100 hours this morning to look for them."

Shield Number 3456 glanced at his timepiece and listened with only half an ear. It read 2000 hours, so he had five hours before going back out on patrol. Was the woman he'd talked to on the street earlier that day connected with the kidnapping? He should mention it to the commander and follow up, but the more he thought about it the more he thought, well, maybe not. The commander was under a lot of pressure to solve the case fast and might blow up and punish him for not reporting it sooner, maybe even take some time off his Lifeline. He was only thirty-three and still had a few years left, so there no sense making waves if he didn't need to. No, he'd just wait until he went back on patrol in five hours and do his own follow up on the woman.

He yawned as the meeting broke up with the final admonishment from the commander ringing in his ears, "Set your laser guns to kill and blast them to kingdom come. I want this over with quick."

Shield 3456 shook his head as he headed for the cafeteria to get something to eat and then try to rest in one of the sleeping pods at the station. It was going to be a long night.

While Commander Langer was wrapping up his meeting, Quinn, his family, and Jen were making their way down the front stairs of the building where they'd been hiding. He checked his timepiece. It read 2030 hours. Darkness had set in, and he was nervous. He adjusted his long hair wig and put on his oxygen mask. Karen and Jen did the same with their masks, pulling them on over their hair, now dyed black. When they were secure, Jen helped Matt with his. Quinn was glad that they all had to wear them because the masks covered their faces. He had no doubt the WOSP, or Shields, as they were sometime called by the citizens, would be out looking for them.

SOMETHING BETTER

At bottom of the steps, he held up a hand. "One last check. Everyone have everything they need?"

Karen and Jen both nodded. Matt, spoke softly, "Yes, Daddy."

Karen came to her husband's side and looked around the corner of the stairwell. The street was dimly lit and empty except for a few citizens hurrying by. "I think the best thing to do is wait here for a bus," she said. "If we can grab one to take us to the outskirts of The City, we'll be safe."

"I think that's our best plan," Quinn said, "It'll get us away from here faster than walking." He knelt down to look Matt in the eye, "Hey there, buddy, from now on while we're outside you need to be very quiet, okay?"

He nodded solemnly and didn't say anything, immediately doing as he was told. In spite of the tense situation Quinn smiled and hugged his son, thinking once more how glad he was their little family was finally all together.

Jen had been keeping a lookout and her sudden gasp startled them all, "Oh, my god."

"What?" Karen made a move to join her, but Jen held out her hand.

"Stay back," she whispered. "I just saw two Shields come around the corner at the far end of the block. They're walking toward us!"

"Damn," Karen swore. She risked a quick peek, "They must be on patrol. I wonder if they're looking for us."

Quinn whispered, "This stairwell is pretty much in shadow. Let's crouch down under the steps and stay quiet and wait for them to go by."

The four of them silently moved under the stairs and waited. Unfortunately, while they were hidden a bus went by. Quinn made eye contact with Karen, both of them thinking the same thing, *there goes our chance.*

A few minutes later the Shields strolled by, flashing lights into recessed areas. They weren't paying much attention, however, talking instead about what they were going to do with their next paycheck. In a few minutes they were out of sight, having turned the corner at the end of the block.

Quinn stepped from their hiding place, took a quick look around and then turned to Karen, "They're gone. What do you think? Should we still risk waiting for a bus?"

Karen checked her timepiece. "It's 2100 hours, just three hours to midnight. It's getting late. I'm not sure how often the buses will continue to run past here. "

Jen spoke up. "I'm worried what will happen when the Shields get serious about looking for us, if not now, soon. Maybe we should make a run for it."

Karen looked at Quinn, both thinking the same thing; it was five miles to the outskirts of The City marked by an abandoned mine that was now used for food storage. It was heavily guarded, but the land beyond was an uninhabited wasteland. If they could get past the storage facility, they'd be safe.

Karen looked at her husband. "You decide," she said.

Quinn looked at Matt. A few days ago, all he'd wanted was spend more time with his son. Then he'd found out that some of the young children the in regional dormitory where Matt was being raised were routinely being abused by a few of the caretakers in charge. He'd made a snap decision to take Matt, acting on emotion and love rather than rational thought, and it had changed the course of their lives forever.

Now, Karen and Jen were involved. If they went back and gave themselves up, they'd be punished, probably killed. Besides, what would they be going back to? The life they'd had, Quinn as an engineer and Karen and Jen as a microbiologist for Millennium Microbial, well, that was really no life at all when you stopped to think about it. He didn't know what lay ahead, but it had to be better than what they were coming from. Plus, they'd at least be together as a family. For a while, anyway. That counted for something as far as he was concerned. Something big.

Quinn made his decision and looked at the three sets of eyes staring hopefully at him and said, trying to sound more confident than he felt. "Let's not risk the buses. Let's make a run for it."

Karen came to him and gave him a reassuring hug and said, "Good move."

Jen gave him the universal 'thumbs up' sign and nodded her head in the affirmative. "I agree."

So that was the plan, although running was a bit of a stretch for what they did that night. Walking was more like it, but walk they did, for five miles though the fetid, semi-deserted streets all the way to the outskirts of The City and the abandoned mine called the Regional Food Storage Facility.

An hour after midnight, at 0100, a force of nearly one-thousand Shields was deployed to hunt down and kill the four fugitives. Shield 3456 was among them and he and his assigned partner for the operation went back to where he had talked to the woman earlier that day.

They arrived at the three-story building at 0130 hours. "I'll search inside, you keep watch on the street," he told Shield 8901, a young recruit.

"Okay, sir."

Shield 3456 searched the first two floors and found no trace of anyone having been in the building. He was starting to think he was mistaken to think that the young woman he'd talked with earlier that day was anyone to worry about, but then he went to the third floor. There he found evidence that people had recently used the space: an empty water bottle, some food wrappers and spots on the floor that looked like dye.

He was about ready to call in the information when he stopped himself. *What will Commander Langer say*, he wondered. He didn't have to wonder long because he knew exactly what the commander would say. He would berate Shield 3456 for being negligent and maybe even demote him to teach him a lesson, not to mention take at least a week off his lifeline. No, he couldn't take that chance. Better to forget it ever happened and let the whole thing blow over. Besides, for all he knew, the young woman had nothing to do with the guy who kidnapped the little kid.

Downstairs he found the new recruit conscientiously keeping an eye on the street. *He'll make a good officer one day*, Shield 3456 thought to himself. *Probably a lot better than me.*

"Okay," he said, stepping through the entrance and taking a left onto the sidewalk, "Let get going."

SOMETHING BETTER

"Find anything?"

"Not a thing," he said, checking the time. It was 0200 hours. "The building's completely empty. Let's check the next block over."

Quinn and Karen and Jen and Matt had found a pile of concrete slabs to hide behind. They were about one-hundred yards from the chain link fence that surrounded the Region Food Storage Facility. The land beyond was a bleak desert devoid of any human inhabitation. The facility was lit up like daylight and there was one main entrance with transport carriers traveling in and out non-stop. Armed security forces patrolled the perimeter. The place was guarded like a military compound. It looked not only menacing but dangerous.

Quinn shrugged off his pack and the others did the same. His timepiece read 0230 hours. Karen took out a bottle of water for them to share, and they all took off their masks to drink. The water was refreshing on their parched throats, and it felt good to rest.

"What are we going to do, now?" Jen asked.

Karen looked at Quinn. "What do you think?"

"I don't know. There's a lot of..." he was going to say there's a lot of people around, but something stopped him. "Hey," he said, taking a deep breath. "I can breathe pretty good without my mask on."

Karen and Jen and Matt reacted the same way. It was true. Away from the heart of The City it seemed the air was better, less poisonous, easier to take in. The three adults smiled at each other, each of them thinking it was nice least one good thing had happened. Maybe it was a good sign.

They continued to share the water. Jen said, "We should probably keep our oxygen masks handy, though, just to be on the safe side. Right, Karen?" Jen turned to face her friend.

Karen had been quietly thinking. "What? Oh, yeah, sure," she said, distracted.

"What's up?" Quinn asked. Karen was a scientist with a brilliant mind. If she was thinking, it usually was a good thing.

"I was just thinking about how to get beyond the guards and how to get out of here. I think the further we get from The City, the better off we'll be."

Matt had been following the conversation with interest. The more time he spent with his mom and dad, the better he felt. "What's up, Mom. What's your idea?" he asked his little voice squeaking in anticipation.

Karen smiled and hugged him. Then she said to Quinn and Jen, "Sometimes the easiest solution is the best one. We really have no choice, do we?"

"Yeah," Quinn said, hesitantly, "I suppose…," He was unsure where she was going with this, "What are you thinking?

Karen smiled and looked to Quinn and Matt and Jen, "I think the choice is easy. We've got to get past the guards and the fence and get out to the land beyond it."

"In other words…," Quinn said.

"We've got to make a run for it."

"It's just a god forsaken desert out there," Jen pointed

out.

"That's okay," Karen said, looking around at the huge facility and all the armed guards on patrol, "We've got no other choice."

And, in the end, they all agreed, it was the best plan.

So that's what they did.

JIM BATES

SOMETHING BETTER

-

Chapter Eight

Escape

BUCK BENSON, BADGE #4455, was security shift leader for the Regional Food Storage Facility. One of his main jobs was overseeing the twenty-three workers who manned the twenty-three control panels that received video feed from four thousand seven hundred fifty-six sensors located inside and outside of the eighty-acre complex. It was a lot to keep track of, especially at night when roving packs of wild dogs frequently tried to break in and steal food. So, when he received a personal call from his boss, general Rawlings, he subconsciously stood at attention and listened.

"Benson, you've got to keep on your toes tonight. The World Order Security Police are going nuts back in The

City."

"What's wrong, sir?"

"Some idiots kidnapped their kid and are making a run for it."

"Kidnapped their kid?"

"It's complicated."

Benson wasn't paid to think, although the statement struck him as odd. Instead, he asked,

"Heading our way, sir?"

"No one knows, but Commander Langer is up in arms. Orders are 'Shoot to kill.' In fact, his exact words are 'Blast them to kingdom come.'"

"A couple of parents and their kid? That seems a little drastic, doesn't it, sir?" The stony quiet on the other end of the line told Benson all he needed to know. "Sorry, sir. We'll keep a lookout."

"You do that, Benson, and remember..."

"Shoot to kill, sir?"

"To kingdom come."

"Okay, got it."

Benson disconnected and checked the time. 0230 hours. Three hours before sunrise. A lot could happen between now and then. He went to the intercom and got the attention of the twenty-three computer operators under his command. "Listen up everyone. Keep on the lookout for some kidnappers. Two or three adults and one child. If you see anything suspicious let me know. I'll take it from there."

Exactly what Buck would do if the kidnappers were

found he didn't know, and he hoped to God he wouldn't have to find out either.

Behind their pile of concrete blocks, Quinn, Karen, Jen, and Matt were resting up for what they hoped would be their final dash to freedom.

"Okay," Quinn said, nervously fiddling with his oxygen mask in his lap and sipping from his water bottle, "lets' go through the plan one more time."

Karen reached over and took the mask from him and set it aside. "Hopefully, we won't need these much longer," she said. "Maybe if we beyond the perimeter we'll be able to discard them all together. Who knows what we'll find that'll be different out there?" Karen was understood science. "My guess? Probably a lot." She turned to Quinn. "Okay. You were saying…"

Quinn had been listening with interest, thinking, not for the first time how glad he was Karen was with him. He was positive if it had just been him, by now he and Matt would have been already caught and at least he would be sitting in prison somewhere. If, that was, he was still alive.

He shook the image from his mind. "Okay, here's what we'll do," he drew a line in the sand, "This is the perimeter. Karen, you saw a chain link fence out there, right?"

"Yeah. The closest section is about fifty yards from us. Just a minute, let me check it again." She pushed an icon on her phone and a binocular application appeared. She got up on her knees and carefully peered over the mound of concrete blocks and scanned back and forth. "The fence is in pretty rough shape. It goes to the right all the way to the entryway where the transport carriers come in and out. There's a couple of guard stations there."

"What's to the left?" Quinn asked.

Karen scanned back the other way. The wind, which has been calm all evening, suddenly picked up, blowing gusts of sand over the barren land. Quinn bent over Matt and covered his head with his body, protecting the little boy from the stinging pellets.

Karen sat back down. "There's nothing out there. It's like a desert."

"How far does the fence go?" Jen asked. She brushed her hair out of her face, uncapped a freshwater bottle and gave it to Karen to drink.

"It goes forever, it looks like. Miles and miles." She took the water and drank. But there's good news."

"What's that?" Both Quinn and Jen at the same time.

"The fence is basically falling apart."

Quinn grinned. "Well, that's good. All we've got to do is get across this open area, find a hole to climb through and we'll be free."

Karen was skeptical. "Maybe. Getting across that space will be hard. I don't like that we don't see anyone patrolling. I'll bet they've got security cameras all over the place."

Matt, who had been quietly listening, suddenly spoke up, "You mean we're trapped here?" Tears welled up in his eyes.

Quinn held his son and looked at Karen with the unspoken question on his lips, *Are we?*

SOMETHING BETTER

Karen quickly smiled and said, primarily for Matt's benefit, "No, we aren't trapped we'll find a way."

And just as she spoke a loud siren went off. It could only mean one thing; a security camera had spotted them. They'd been discovered.

Quinn jumped to his feet. "They've seen us. Let's get out of here." He grabbed his pack and Matt and started running for the fence, Karen, and Jen right behind each struggling to put on their packs. Karen risked a quick look over her shoulder and gasped. Charging toward them was a group of about ten security guards. There was a flash of light and a rock next to her exploded. They were shooting at them. "Run!" she screamed. "Faster."

Back at the security bay, Buck Benson watched the events unfolding on the video monitors and smiled to himself. He'd trusted his instincts and his instincts had been correct. One of the sensors located on the perimeter had detected a higher level of heat concentration than normal and he'd sent a small squad out to investigate. Watching the chase unfold before his eyes in real time told him all he needed to know; there had been people out there. Were they the fugitives everyone was so eager to kill? Probably. He'd find out soon enough because he'd give the same order to his men that had been given to him, "Shoot to kill. Blast them to kingdom come." So that's what he told them to do.

He sighed a contented sigh and checked the time. 0330 hours. It'd all be over with soon, before sunrise even. Good. He was looking forward to a nice hearty breakfast to celebrate.

Buck was just sitting down at his computer to begin

writing his report when the phone rang. He glanced at the screen and frowned. It was Anderson, his squad leader.

"Benson here. What's up?"

Anderson's voice was shaky. "Sir, I don't know what happened."

Benson sat up, suddenly on edge. He could hear the wind blowing in the background of Anderson's phone but that wasn't all he heard. He could also hear Anderson's voice loud and clear, and he didn't like the tone of it one little bit. "What going on out there, Anderson? You better have good news for me," he threatened. The silence on the other end of the line told him all he needed to know. "Anderson!" he screamed. "What happened?"

Anderson had a tough time talking because his mouth had suddenly gone bone dry. He feared Benson and what the possible repercussions might be, none of them good. After a few moments he was finally able to work up enough saliva and courage to talk, "We were closing in on them, sir, and suddenly the weirdest thing happened."

Oh, no, Benson put his hand over his eyes and shook his head. This was not good. He asked anyway, "What?"

"They disappeared."

"Disappeared?" Benson thundered and slammed his fist down on the computer console. "You're crazy. I saw you on the monitor. You weren't more than a hundred yards away."

"I know. I don't understand it myself, sir. One minute they were here, the next moment they were gone."

"Stay right there, Anderson. I'm coming down."

Ten minutes later Benson joined Anderson and the rest

of the squad. They searched and searched but couldn't find a trace of the fugitives. It was as if the wind had carried them away.

In a way it had. As they had toward the fence, Karen spied a hole in the chain link and called out, "Come on. Hurry up. Follow me."

A strong wind was blowing, blasting swirling sand all around that was so dense it obscured the sight of the security guards pursuing them. Karen led them through the hole confident that the gusting wind would obliterate their tracks, which it did. They stopped for a moment and quickly put their oxygen masks on for protection from the sand and continued on.

Beyond the fence the land they found themselves in was treacherous. To make matters worse, away from the bright lights of the facility the night was dark, so they had to make their way slowly, stumbling frequently over rocks and broken boulders. Finally, they came upon a small rise about a mile into the desert. They climbed to the far side, plopped down, took off their masks and then lay sprawled in the dirt exhausted.

Matt recovered first and sat up, "Wow, Daddy, that was fun."

Quinn struggled to a sitting position and grinned at his son, "I'm not sure fun is the word I'd use, but at least we're safe."

"For now, anyway," Jen said. She busied herself getting some water and snacks out of her pack and passed them around. Then she looked at Karen. "What's up?"

Karen had her binocular app running. The wind had abated enough to see better. She was lying flat on the crest of the hill scanning back and forth, watching the security guards a mile away. "They're all wandering around, trying to find our tracks I guess."

"The wind blew them away, right?"

"Yeah, it did. I just hope they don't come past the perimeter and start seriously searching for us."

Jen shivered, not so much from the cold, but from nerves. "Me, too."

"Mommy, are we going to do anymore running? I had good time doing that."

Despite the seriousness of their predicament, Karen cracked a smile at her son, "Hopefully not, sweetheart." Then she looked at Quinn. Even though his actions had gotten them into the mess they were in, she wouldn't trade this moment in time for anything. They were a family, and they were together. That was the main thing. "What about it, Quinn? Got a plan?"

Quinn turned his gaze away from the facility they'd just escaped from and focused his attention in the other direction, the grey light of dawn spreading over the wasteland they'd soon be traveling through. Could they make it? The answer was simple if not frightening they had no choice. They'd have to.

He looked affectionately at his little band of fugitives. He was proud of them all, as well as of himself, but they were all tired and need to rest. "Let's take a break and have some water and food. Then we'll head out."

"That's good, Daddy," Matt said, turning toward Jen, "I'm

hungry."

Jen opened up an energy bar and gave it to the little boy and then made a motion to Karen who came over to join her. "Bad news," Jen said.

"What?"

"We're low in food. We're going through it faster than I thought we would."

"Damn." Karen turned to Quinn. "You hear that?"

"Wha...What? Low on food," he said, distractedly. "Yeah, I heard."

Karen went to stand next to him. "What's up?"

Quinn pointed, "Look at that."

Jen and Matt joined them, so they were all looking.

"What is it, Daddy?"

"Yeah," Jen said. "What is it?"

Quinn said, "Karen. Use your binocular app. What do you think?"

Early dawn was casting dim light into the sky, making it a little easier to see. After a minute she said, "That tall, dark, wall looking line on the horizon? There's only one thing it can be. I think it's a mountain range." she said, quietly. "They're way out there maybe twenty miles."

Quinn looked at her, "Do you think we should try to get to them. Maybe we'll be safe there."

Karen turned and looked behind her. The security forces had given up and were heading back to the facility. For now, their little group appeared to be safe. She turned toward the mountains looming far in the distance. Quinn's idea was their only option, but it was a good one. They might be able find someplace safe to live in them and start a new life. "Yeah, I think that's what we should do," she said. "Let's head for the mountains."

"All right," Quinn, agreed, "But first let's rest a little. We've got a long way to go."

SOMETHING BETTER

Chapter Nine

No Man's Land

BY MID-AFTERNOON, Quinn and Karen and Matt and Jen had traveled about five miles west from where they'd escaped through the fence surrounding the food storage warehouse at the edge of The City. They were now making their way across the bleak desert landscape that to them had become known as No Man's Land. Quinn's canvas shoes kicked up dust as he walked. The rocky, sunbaked ground was tearing them up and wouldn't last much longer. Then what would he do? He tried not to think about it and instead focused on the people under his care.

His son Matt had given in to exhaustion, so Quinn was carrying him on his shoulders with one of his shirts draped over the boy's head for protection, both from the sun and the sand. Earlier, he had taken off both his and Matt's long hair wigs and buried them under some rocks. It was hot out, and it felt good to have the off.

A hot wind blew fine, granular particles that bounced off the glass eye-shields of their gas masks. Karen had encouraged them to wear the masks more for protection from the sand than for safety from air pollution like in The City. The further into the desert they traveled, the better the air quality. Still, as Karen told them as they started out on their journey, "We should mask up. Better safe than sorry." So, they did.

The sun had risen hours ago making it easier to see, and Quinn watched Karen and Jen fifty feet in front of him slowly making their way. Their hunched over, shuffling gait, told the whole story: not only was their mood grim, they were also about at the end of their rope. And the mountains in the distance they were heading for weren't getting any closer.

To make matters worse, the dust was clogging the filters in everyone's gas masks making it hard to breathe.

"I hate these things! Let's get rid of them," Jen said, stopping and angerly starting to remove hers.

Karen put out a hand to stop her. "Look, I know they're uncomfortable, but let's leave them on until we get a little further away from The City. You never know what pollutants there are out here." She pointed back behind them. "We've only come about five miles."

Jen stomped her foot, throwing up a cloud of dust. "Fine!" Then she moderated her tone. "Look, I'm sorry. I know you're right. I'm just tired. Let's at least rest and have some water." She pointed toward Matt as Quinn came up to them. "He's being a real trooper, but I'm sure he could use a break."

Matt took the shirt off from his head. "I'm okay," he said from his dad's shoulders. Then he started coughing. "I am a little thirsty, though."

"I think we could all use a break," Quinn said. "Let's sit over there in the shade of that boulder."

He set Matt down and took off the boy's gas mask, then his own, while Karen and Jen did the same. Then the three adults took off their back packs and sprawled out on the hard ground, utterly spent.

After resting a minute, Jen started to revive a little. She sat up and looked around. "I think No Man's Land is a perfect name for this place." She took a bottle of water from her pack and handed it to Karen. "It's the ugliest place I've ever seen."

"Yeah, even more so than The City," Karen said, unscrewing the cap and taking a drink. "It's hot, too." She gave the bottle to Matt who drank it all in about half a minute.

"Thanks, Mom," he gasped. "I guess I was pretty thirsty."

Jen handed a bottle to Quinn who took a sip and then and splashed a handful of water on his face and his head to cool off. His hand came away filthy from the dust. He rubbed it on his pants leg and commented, "At least we made it past the security guards."

"Yeah, but now what?" Jen asked. She pointed west toward the mountain range about fifteen miles away. "That's a long way to walk, especially in these conditions."

"I know," Karen said, cradling Matt who was nodding off into an exhausted sleep even though it was barely noon. She turned to Quinn. "What do you think? Can we make it?"

"We've got to. We have no other choice."

He shielded his eyes and looked out over the brown, burnt out wasteland. Desolate was putting it mildly. He saw no living things. The land was hostile and barren, covered in rocks and sand and gravel, with the only visual relief boulders like the one they were resting next to and the occasional hill and rock outcropping.

To the west the desert slopped toward the foothills with the mountains rising tall behind them. Quinn was looking in that direction wondering if they had it in them to make the arduous journey when he spotted a plume of dust rising in the distance. Something was coming toward them. Karen saw it, too.

"Look," she pointed.

"What is it?" Jen stood up, squinting her eyes against the relentless sun before shielding them like Quinn was having to do.

"I don't know," Quinn said, "But I have a feeling it can't be good." He pointed to a nearby outcropping of rocks. "Let's climb up there just to be on the safe side."

"And hide," Karen added.

"Yeah. That, too," Quinn said, grimacing, trying unsuccessfully to cover his mounting apprehension.

They put their masks on. Matt was so tired Quinn had to carry him. Karen and Jen hurried ahead, scrambling over rocks and large boulders as they climbed to the top of the outcropping before realizing that Quinn needed help with Matt, so they went back down to assist him. When they were all together, they crouched down, breathing hard, about thirty feet above the floor of the desert.

Angerly Jen pulled off her mask. "I can barely breathe," she said, sucking in air.

Karen took off the filter assembly. "It's clogged again with dust. Let me put a new one in for you." She reached into her pack, took out a clean filter and put it in before handing it back. "Here you go."

While Karen was helping Jen, Quinn was watching the approaching cloud of dust. "Karen, let me have your phone." She handed it over and Quinn switched on the binocular function before peering through it. "Geez, look at this." He handed the phone to her.

Karen looked and her heart jumped, "Oh, man."

"What is it?" Jen asked.

"Wild dogs," Karen said, giving the phone back to Quinn. "It looks like a pack of about ten of them."

Jen didn't hesitate. She looked around and picked up a fist sized rock, then started collecting more. "Damn it. We didn't come this far to get eaten by a bunch of dogs. Let's get ready for them."

Karen and Matt jumped into action with Jen, and the three of them began collecting rocks and stacking them into a pile.

Quinn kept an eye on the approaching pack. "They're moving fast. Yeah, I'd say there are about ten of them. At least. The leader is a big white one. Looks kind of like that wolf we saw in the biodome exhibit a few weeks ago." He looked at his son. "Remember?"

"Yeah, I do," Matt said excitedly. "That was fun."

It had been fun. Now here they were, making their escape and looking for a better life. Quinn wasn't going to let a pack of wild dog's ruin that dream.

He watched them approaching and said, "They're getting closer. Closer."

Karen took the binoculars from him. "I can see them, Quinn." She pointed and he looked. They were only a quarter of a mile away.

Jen selected two rocks from the pile and held one in each hand. "I'm ready."

Quinn and Karen did the same.

"You stay behind us," Karen told Matt. Then, seeing the disappointment in his eyes at not being able to help, added, "You can hand us rocks, okay?"

His face brightened, "Okay, Mom."

Quinn watched the pack veer toward them. "They must have picked up our scent." He gripped his rocks tightly. "Get ready."

The dogs picked up speed. The hunt was on. The leader was silent but fast and he out distanced the others, his tongue lolling out the side of its jaws, lips pulled back revealing huge, sharp canines. The rest of the pack crowded in behind him and broke into insane howling.

The big white dog leaped from the desert floor to a large boulder at the base of the outcropping and began climbing steadily toward them, his eyes bright with the promise of fresh meat. The howling and fevered baying of the rest of the pack filled the air like deranged banshees as they clawed over rocks right behind their leader, driven mad by hunger and the scent of their prey.

It was terrifying watching the ravenous pack climb toward them, but Jen wasn't going to let fear get the better of them. She took charge and turned to Quinn and Karen. "Follow my lead," she said. They both held their rocks tightly and nodded a silent 'okay.' She turned her attention to the pack. "Okay, now, hold it. Hold it. Hold it," she said, watching as howling pack climbed closer and closer. Finally, when the lead dog was only fifteen feet away, she leaped from her hiding place and screamed, "Get out of here!" She heaved her rock with all her might, then watched in utter surprise and amazement as it hit the leader square in the middle of the forehead, cracked open his skull and dropped him in his tracks, killing him instantly.

The rest of the pack appeared stunned as they gathered around him, sniffing at the dead corpse. Jen didn't hesitate. She hurled her other rock and took the ones Matt handed her and threw them as well. Quinn and Karen joined her, the three of them raining rocks down on the pack until they ran off, leaving their leader dead and broken.

"Yea!" Matt yelled, jumping up and down. "We won. We won."

Quinn grinned at Karen and Jen, and they grinned back. Yes, they had.

To celebrate they all took off their gasmasks and Jen handed out water for them to drink as they watched the pack run off, continuing in the direction they'd been heading.

"Must be going for the storage facility," Jen said. "I'll bet to steal some food. They're probably starving."

"Speaking of..." Karen said, pointing at Jen's pack. "You're in charge of our supplies. How are we doing on food and water?"

Jen checked. "All we've got are energy bars, enough for a couple of days. Water is what we really need, especially to cross this desert." She looked to the west toward the mountains. Heat waves simmered off the sand. Dust devils danced across the foreboding landscape. The sun beat down unmercifully. "We'll have to conserve how much we drink and be judicious if we plan on making it." She turned to Quinn. "What do you think? Three or four days to get there?"

"Yeah, that'd be my guess." He looked at Karen. "What do you think?"

"I think we can do it, but we're going to have to keep moving slowly. We don't want to get too worn out." With her eyes she indicated toward Matt. Quinn got her meaning. The journey was going to be hard on the little guy, not to mention the rest of them.

Quinn slapped his hands together as if sealing the deal. "Okay, then," he said. "That's what we'll do. We've got to get across this desert and get away from this heat and into the mountains. Hopefully once we get there, we'll be able for find more food and water."

"What happens if we don't, Dad?" Matt asked.

"Karen hugged the little boy. "Don't worry," she said. "We've made it this far. We can make it to the mountains." She looked at her husband. "Right, Quinn?"

"Sure," he said, getting up and helping Matt to his feet.

SOMETHING BETTER

"We've come too far to give up now."

Karen and Jen stood and joined them, and they all clasped hands spontaneously in a show of solidarity.

They decided to save the water Jen had handed out for later, and she packed the bottles away. Then they all secured their gas masks, carefully climbed down the outcropping, and started off across the desert. They walked the rest of the day, but the mountains never seemed to get any closer. That was okay. They'd beaten back the wild dogs. They'd escaped the security forces and made it out of The City. And, most importantly, they were alive. That was the main thing. Even though they all knew there would be more obstacles to overcome and more challenges to face in the near future, for right now, right then and there, they all felt the same way; they were invincible. They could survive anything.

JIM BATES

SOMETHING BETTER

Chapter Ten

The Mountains

QUINN AND KAREN rested while Jen scouted ahead. They had been traversing the foothills for the last day but didn't seem to be getting any closer to the mountain range rising in front of them. They were so close they felt they could reach out and touch them, but, of course, they couldn't, and their plight was wearing everyone down.

"How's your water supply holding up?" Quinn asked.

Karen took the plastic bottle out of her pack and showed him. "Half empty. Or half full according to you." She attempted a smile through her cracked lips but was unsuccessful. The three-day hike across No Man's Land had taken its toll on her generally positive disposition.

Quinn showed her his bottle. "Same," he said, and didn't even try to make a joke. He was too exhausted.

Done in by their arduous journey, Matt had fallen asleep in his father's lap moments after they'd stopped to rest. Dust devils blew past in an endless parade reminding them that if they didn't find water soon, they would die. They'd been out of food for over a day.

"We should conserve water even more than we are," Karen said, raising her bottle to take a drink before putting it down, screwing the cap on and putting it away. She hadn't touched a drop. "I'll save it for Matt," she whispered to Quinn.

At the sound of his name, Matt stirred and sat up. Blinking and rubbing his eyes he asked, "Where's Jen?" They'd become fast friends in the five days since they'd met in The City and begun their journey together.

Quinn rubbed his son's head, mussing up his red hair in a show of affection. "She went on up ahead," he pointed. "See, she's out there."

Jen had walked along the spur of a rocky outcropping and was about a hundred yards away. As they watched, she turned and shouted. "Hey, you guys. Come here. Come quick. I think I see something."

Instead of waiting, she jogged back as the three of them hurried to meet her. Quinn was carrying Matt on his back.

They met halfway. "What is it?" he asked.

"I see rocks piled up out there. Like a symbol or signal of some sort." She motioned and began walking, "Come on."

Quinn and Karen followed her to the first pile. "Look," she pointed. "See what I mean? I wonder what they are?" She was showing them a two-foot-tall stack of flat rocks set one on top of the other with the larger ones, about two feet across, at the bottom, and smaller ones placed on top of each other.

Karen said, "I've read about these." She bent down and studied the pyramid shaped structure. "It's called a cairn. They're used to mark a path over rocky ground."

Quinn set Matt down. "So, you don't get lost?" Matt asked. He'd been following the conversation closely.

"That's right," his mom said.

"So, someone put them there?"

Quinn, Karen, and Jen all looked at the five-year-old. They could see it in his eyes, the dull stare of exhaustion was replaced by a bright, almost a lively glimmer; a glimmer of what they all suddenly felt. Something they hadn't felt for a few days. Hope.

"Yes," his mother said, "Someone put them there."

"Wow," Matt exclaimed.

Jen had another thought. "On the other hand, we don't know anything about whoever built them. They might be friendly, they might not."

"She's right," Karen said. "We should be careful."

"But we should follow them, right?" Quinn asked.

"Yeah, we should," Karen answered him.

Jen added. "We really don't have any other choice, do we?"

"No, we don't," Quinn nodded grimly. "Let's go." He set Matt back on his shoulders and off they went.

The cairns were spaced out about every hundred yards or so. Sometimes it was hard to find the next one, and more than once they got off in the wrong direction. Crossing No Man's Land had been hard going and the dry ground had torn up their shoes, making walking difficult. Since yesterday, when they'd begun climbing into the foothills, the land was still dry and sunbaked, but hillier, and they had to do more climbing which further ruined their shoes and made walking even more difficult. The closer they got to the mountains, the hillier the land became and the harder it was to make progress.

After following the cairns for most of the afternoon they were all exhausted.

"Let's stop here and rest," Quinn said. He took Matt off his shoulders, and they plopped down on the rocky ground. The others gratefully joined them.

"Dad, I'm thirsty," Matt said and coughed a little. "My throat is really dry."

Quinn gave him his water bottle and watched as the little boy drank half of what was left, which wasn't much. He smiled, though, when Matt handed it back and said, "Here, Dad. I saved some for you."

"Thanks, buddy," he grabbed his son for a quick one-armed hug and took a sip. He was nearing the last of his water.

Karen and Jen each took a sip from theirs, trying to conserve. They, too, were on their last bottles. They'd finished off the last of their energy bars the day before. If they didn't find food and more importantly, water, soon, their fate was sealed.

Quinn looked back from where they'd come from, back toward No Man's Land and The City they'd escaped to build a better life. Exactly what that life was going to look like, Quinn had no idea, but he'd never second guess himself for the risk they'd taken. At least now his family was together, that was the main thing. But it would all be for nothing if they didn't find water soon.

Karen got up and pulled on her backpack. "We need to get going."

Jen joined her. "I'm glad we don't have to wear those gas masks anymore. They were started to bug me."

In spite of their dire situation, Karen smiled. "I know. You weren't happy at all."

The further they'd traveled from The City, the better the air had become. The dust storms weren't as prevalent either. So yesterday Karen pronounced the air safe for them all to breathe. "You mean we can ditch the gas masks?" Jen had asked, grinning from ear to ear, and removing hers and tossing it aside. "It's about time."

"Yes, but let's keep them with us," Karen said, reaching down, picking it up and handing it back to her. "You never know when they might come in handy for something."

"Yeah, I guess you're right," Jen said, and put it in her backpack.

Yesterday, the cleaner air had been a morale booster, but now, having no food and running out of water, the good mood of the group was starting to fade.

Quinn had an idea. "Jen, why don't you scout up ahead like before and check out where the cairns are leading? We'll follow along with Matt."

Jen was happy to have the responsibility. Of all of them, as the journey progressed, she was turning out to be the one in the best shape and was happy to accommodate. "Sure. Consider it done."

Quinn and Karen watched her trot over the rocky ground before Quinn lifted Matt to his shoulders and they began following behind, picking their way slowly over the irregular ground. The hills surrounding them were getting steeper. The sun was getting low in the sky behind the mountain range in front of them. Dusk was setting in and it would soon be dark with the night bringing colder temperatures. They'd have to consider making camp and figuring out a way to get through the night while trying not to think about how cold they were and the food they didn't have.

Suddenly they heard a shout. Jen appeared on the top of a low rise in front of them and waved, "Hey guys, come here. Hurry!"

"What is it?" Karen yelled, picking up her pace and taking Quinn's hand, pulling him along.

"Good news. The trail goes into a canyon. I've got a feeling there might be water in it."

Quinn and Karen joined her and looked to where she was pointing. The trail veered away from the direction they'd been traveling and cut to the left, dropping down into what looked to be a shady canyon.

Quinn didn't have to think, "Let's go and check it out." They scrambled down the steep decline, slipping and sliding all the way.

Once at the bottom they noticed the air was remarkably cooler and immediately their spirits revived. The sides of the canyon were steep and blocked out most of the sun, but after walking a short way along a sandy trail they found a pool of spring fed water. After drinking their fill and filling their bottles, they made camp for the night. As the sun set, they huddled together for warmth against the cold night air and slept fitfully. Even though their thirst was quenched, hunger pangs were strong; they'd been without food for nearly two days and needed to find some soon.

At dawn, the next day the little group was up and moving. They followed the cairns, which after a few hours led them out of the cool canyon, up a steep hill and into the warmth of the sun. The stream disappeared below the hill they were standing on.

"I'm going to scout ahead," Jen said.

"Go for it," Quinn told her, and not for the first time was glad for Jen's take charge attitude.

Both he and Karen watched, resting with Matt, as Jen scampered ahead. They were just getting ready to follow when she came running back. Breathlessly she said, "Guys. I think we've made it. I can see a beautiful valley out there. It's only a few miles away. I think the canyon led us through the mountains. We didn't have to climb them. Who knows how many days it saved us?"

"Are you sure?" Quinn asked.

"Who cares?" Karen said. "Let's go see."

Jen led them back to where she'd been. She'd followed a cairn to the edge of a steep hill that fell away below them. "Look," she pointed. At the bottom they could see where the creek had reappeared.

"My god," Karen said. "I don't believe it."

"But it's true," Jen pointed further. The creek followed a

meandering path and then spilled out into a valley that looked to be about six miles away. And the best part? It wasn't like the brown desert they'd been traveling through for the last five days. Not at all. This land was green.

"It's beautiful," Karen said, smiling. She hugged Quinn and Matt, and then hugged Jen. "We made it!"

"We've still got a way to go," Quinn pointed out. "Plus, we don't have any food."

"He's right," Jen said. "You guys come along. I'll keep scouting up ahead. Maybe I can find some berries or something."

Quinn and Karen watched their friend climb down the hill and begin following the creek on its way to the valley. Before coming after her, though, they sat down with Matt to let the little boy rest before heading out.

"Are we really going to be saved, Dad?" he asked, snuggling with his mom. "Really?"

"Yes, we are," Quinn said, not adding the last part of what he was going to say, which was, "I think." Truth be told, he really didn't know. In his heart, however, and for the good of them all, he hoped they were finally through the worst of their journey. He really did.

Next to him Karen took his hand, "You did a good thing, Quinn, kidnapping Matt and getting us out of The City. At the time, I wasn't sure if it was a wise thing to do, but, in the end, if it wasn't the wisest thing to do, it certainly was the right thing to do." She paused and smiled and hugged both Quinn and Matt tightly. "Look at us. We're together. We're a family."

Quinn grinned. "My turn." And he hugged both Karen

and Matt. Yes, they were. They were a family, who could now live the way they wanted, just like he'd always imagined them doing.

Hopefully.

He was feeling so good, he didn't hear Matt the first time until his son poked him in the arm. "Dad?"

"What?" he had bent his head to organize his backpack before following Jen.

"Dad, look. It's Jen."

"Good. We'll keep our eyes on her and follow her in just a minute." He wasn't looking, but, instead, was busying himself with the flap on his pack.

"Um, Quinn," Karen said, standing up. Something in her tone made Quinn stop his packing. He stood up and joined her.

"What?"

"Look." She pointed.

Quinn looked. "Oh, my god," he said.

"Yeah," Karen looked at him. "Now what'll we do?"

He looked back at her. Then out to where Jen was, "I don't know. You have any ideas."

"Nope."

Karen took out her phone and turned on the binocular application and watched Jen approach. But she wasn't alone. She was with a man, a guy about six and a half feet tall wearing a loose-fitting white cotton shirt and pants with a leather satchel strapped across his chest. He had long black hair and a swarthy complexion. Even at a great distance Karen could see he had brilliant white teeth. She knew because she could see him smiling. So was Jen. They both were. They were talking, and every now and then Jen laughed at something the man said.

Quinn turned to Karen and said, "What do you think of that?"

"What I think is that Jen's found a friend."

Jen had, indeed, found a friend.

"Welcome to our land," the stranger said, a little while later, walking up to Quinn and Karen and Matt and extending his hand for all three of them to shake. Which all three of them did. "Let me introduce myself. I am Aaron and," he pointed behind him to the green valley, "my people and I are from down there. We would be very happy to have you all come live with us."

He explained that he was one of nearly four hundred people who were living in the valley; people who over the years had escaped the city and begun living a better life there.

"You're serious?" Quinn asked. "You want us to come and live with you?"

"I am," the friendly, good-natured man said. "I've never been more serious in my life."

"Let's go, Dad," Matt said, obviously smitten with the stranger. "I'm hungry."

Aaron reached into his satchel and pulled out something that smelled delicious. "Here, little man," he said, "Have some of this."

Matt sniffed it and then took a tentative bite. His eyes lit up. "This is good!" And quickly ate it all.

Aaron turned to Quinn and Karen. "It's called bread," he said. "I'll teach you how to make it."

Jen took Aaron by the arm and said to Quinn, "Should we go, then?"

"Yeah, lets," Quinn said.

"Definitely," Karen added.

Matt yelled, "Yippee!"

Quinn hoisted Matt onto his back and Karen took his hand, turned to him and said, "We really did it, Quinn. We made it,"

Quinn smiled back at her, and they embraced. "Yeah, we did."

And off they went, hand and hand, following Jen and Aaron, but they hadn't gone a few steps when Karen frowned and turned to him with a look on her face he'd seen before. The last time was when he'd told her about kidnapping Matt without out a plan. He knew she was wondering something similar right now.

"So now what's the plan?" she asked, squeezing his hand, smiling a little. "What are we going to do now?"

Quinn smiled at her and then happened to catch the motion of a big bird soaring high in the sky above them. He'd never seen one before, but he'd read about them. It was a golden eagle. He pointed, "Look, Karen. It's an eagle."

"It's beautiful," she said. "Maybe a harbinger of things to come?"

"Maybe," Quinn said, as they continued walking together. "Hopefully."

"And, what about a plan?"

"Don't worry," Quinn said and stopping and hugged her. "Between the two of us, we'll think of something."

Karen grinned at him. "Yes, we will."

SOMETHING BETTER

Chapter Eleven

Lost

THEY WERE SITTING side by side in a small park. The sun was shining, and a light breeze blew through the trees and there was a scent of springtime wildflowers in the air. Karen's red hair glistened in the sun, the black dye she'd used for a disguise when they escaped from The City was long gone.

She grinned and hugged Quinn and ran her fingers through his long hair. In addition to growing his beard back, he was also letting his hair grow, and she liked the feel of his dark brown curls. Back in The City he used to keep his head shaved. Now, though, eight months later, things had changed.

"I've never been so happy," she said, and kissed him passionately. "I never thought we'd end up like this."

"It's almost like in a dream, isn't it?" Quinn kissed her in return and rubbed her protruding belly. "And I never thought that we'd ever have another child. How's the little one doing, by the way?"

Karen put her hand over her husbands and gazed into his eyes. "She is doing, fine. Almost eight months along. She's looking forward to meeting her daddy."

"She?"

"Oh, yeah. I can tell."

"That's very cool." Quinn grinned at his wife but was distracted when, nearby, a bird began singing. "Look," Quinn said, reaching for a bird identification book and flipping through it. "I think that's a catbird."

Karen grinned at her easily sidetracked husband. "Pretty voice."

"Yeah, and that tree it's in…I think that's a cottonwood." He consulted another book, one on tree identification. "Yep, it is."

"Good to know," Karen tickled him playfully, then lay back and looked up through the branches of the tree to a cloudless blue sky. She wasn't kidding when she said she'd never been happier. They had been rescued just in time by Aaron, who had led them to the village of Nedlaw on the bank of the Willow River, the same river they had followed out of the mountains. The same river they were now sitting next to.

And life was good. They lived in a small cottage on edge of the village. They had jobs which helped them contribute to the mostly agrarian community. Their son was in school and was making friends. They were together as a family and could live as they wished without the government breathing down their necks. Like Quinn had said, it was a dream come true.

Karen sat up and opened her backpack. "Let have our lunch."

"Great." Quinn opened his pack, "I've brought some black berries and a couple of containers of water."

Karen handed him a honey and apple butter sandwich and Quinn hungerly took a bite. "Man, you make the best bread. Who would have ever thought?"

Karen smiled and nudged him with her elbow. "Hey, I was a scientist, you know, back in the day." But those days were long gone. Now she put her scientific mind to use making wonderfully tasty bread as well as working as a panel technician at the solar energy farm that helped provide power to the village.

Quinn savored his sandwich and watched the river. It was about forty feet wide and rushing rapidly due to yesterday's rains. Downstream about a mile he could just make out a series of low buildings from the village. Another couple of miles on the other side was the dam where the grindstone was located for the watermill. It's where Quinn worked assisting the miller in processing the wheat grown in the valley. Wheat flour was the staple of the community and Quinn was honored to be part of the labor force used in producing it.

"Have you talked to Jen lately?" he asked, munching on a handful of black berries.

"Yeah. I saw her and Aaron yesterday at the market. She's doing really well. She likes working as a teacher's aide at the school."

"What do you think? Are she and Aaron serious?"

"Yeah, I'd say. You can tell. She just shines."

"Well, I'm glad. She's a good person. I'm not sure we would have made it across No Man's Land and the mountains without her."

"Not to mention fighting off the wild dogs."

"Yeah, no kidding." Quinn shook his head. "Who could forget?"

Karen put her arm around his shoulders. "I'm just glad we're here. We've got a good life going."

"We do."

He was about to say more when all of a sudden, the tower bell in the village square began ringing.

"Oh no!" Karen looked to her left. "Wonder what's going on?"

Quinn stood up and helped her to her feet. "Let's pack up our stuff and find out."

It took them about fifteen minutes to get to the park that formed the village square. Jen had been watching for them and waved to get their attention.

"Guys," she ran up to them, "I'm glad you're here. We've got a big problem."

"What do you mean?" Karen asked. Jen rarely got rattled but something was clearly upsetting her.

"What's going on?" Quinn asked.

She looked at them both and said, "There's no way to sugar coat this so I'll be upfront. Matt's gone missing. He wandered off from Shellie's house. She thinks he's up in the hills."

But Matt wasn't.

Earlier in the day, when his parents had decided to go on a picnic, Quinn asked Matt to come along, but he'd begged off, saying, "But, my friend Gary wanted me to go over to his house and play with him."

This was the first Quinn had heard of it. He turned to Karen. "Know anything about this?"

"No." She knelt down so she was eye to eye with her son. "Remember our discussion? We've talked about this. When something unexpected comes up, even if it's going to see a friend, you have to tell us about it."

Matt was contrite, but adamant. "I'm sorry, Mom. But Gary and I talked about it at school. He really wants me to come over. Please can I go?"

Matt had flourished since they'd been living in the village. After being raised under brutal conditions by emotionally cold and distant strangers in a regional operated dormitory in the city, he was growing into a confident, intelligent, and happy boy under the guidance of a patient teacher, and the loving care and devotion of his parents. Quinn and Karen were trying to be careful not to indulge him too much, but in this case, it made sense. Gary was a nice kid, the two of them were the same age, and they were good friends.

Karen looked at Quinn and they nodded to each other. "Okay," Karen said, "You and I and your dad will walk you over to Gary's on the way to our picnic." She smiled and emphasized 'our,' making a joke as she squeezed Quinn's arm, both of them now looking forward to some unexpected time with just the two of them.

"Yippee!" enthused Matt.

Shellie's husband had died of a brain tumor just after Gary was born and she was raising him as a single parent, telling everyone that Jeb had been the love of her life, and no one could replace him. And she is doing a wonderful job with Gary, too, teaching him good values while working as a nursing assistant at the local clinic. She also had a way with cookies and muffins and pies she traded for food and other essentials that she needed. Quinn and Karen referred to Shellie and her son as "Good people" and they happily dropped Matt off and went on their way, walking hand in hand.

After his parents left, Matt and Gary played outside while Shellie kept an eye on them from the kitchen where she was making honey-sugar cookies for the market. She was just mixing in an egg when she heard Gary screaming from the yard. She dropped what she was doing and ran outside where she could see in an instant what was happening. The kids had gotten into a nest of mud wasps that were swarming all over them. Matt had run away, but Gary remained frozen in place, petrified with fear. Shellie ran and grabbed him, brushing wasps off as she hurried inside the cottage to comfort him and administer to his stings.

Left on his own Matt would have been fine playing by himself, but, at that moment, a young dog wandered into the yard. When the little fellow spied Matt, he ran up to him, yipping playfully and wagging its tail.

SOMETHING BETTER

"Oh, what a cute little doggy," Matt said, dropping to the ground to play. He reminded Matt of the dogs they'd seen crossing No Man's Land on their way to the mountains. But this little guy seemed lots friendlier than that pack of vicious wild canines. He was smallish, mostly white with some black marking around his face and floppy ears. Matt giggled as the puppy licked his face. "Oh, you silly little guy." The puppy allowed Matt to pick him up and hold him. "I think I'll call you Joey."

It was an instant bond. When Matt set him down and Joey took off running, Matt didn't think twice. He sped after his new friend, following him out of Shellie's yard, across a field and down a trail through a grove of trees all the way down to the river. When Joey stepped to the edge to get a drink, Matt was right behind him.

"Hey, little guy. You thirsty? I am, too."

Without thinking, Matt stepped off the bank into the water, but the combination of the river's fast current and slippery stones were too much. He lost his footing and fell, pinwheeling his arms in a vain attempt to regain his balance before plunging into the cold, rushing water. Instantly, he was caught up in the raging river and carried downstream, bobbing through the waves, and smashing off rocks as he struggled to stay afloat.

"Help. Help me. Mom. Dad," he yelled, but no one was around to hear him.

No one but Joey.

On the shore, the little dog saw his new friend struggling to stay afloat and didn't hesitate. He leaped into churning waters and fought the current until he was able to swim close enough for Matt to grab hold.

"Joey," Matt called as he enfolded the little dog into his arms and pulled him tightly to his chest. Joey licked Matt's face as together as they were propelled downstream, Joey's buoyancy helping to keep them from sinking. Matt couldn't see it, but only a half a mile away was the dam and the mill with its huge grindstone spinning fast in the rushing river. They were being swept toward it, the icy water sapping Matt's strength as he became weaker by the minute. All he could do was hold on to Joey for dear life.

Upon hearing the news Matt was missing, Quinn and Karen became frantic. While Jen tried to calm them, her friend Aaron came up and quickly explained about Gary and the mud wasps. When he was finished, much to Quinn and Karen's relief, he took charge and said, "Okay, here's what we'll do…"

He separated the villagers into teams of two and had them spread out, sending some toward the foothills, some to search the village and some to comb through the wheat fields outside of town.

Karen gratefully watched the search groups hurrying off, but she was near tears, imploring Quinn, "We've got to find him."

He took her hand, "Let's go back to Shellie's and start from there."

"Good idea," Aaron agreed.

As they made their way to where Matt was last seen, Jen tried to get Karen to focus. "Any idea where he could have gone?"

"None." She turned to Quinn, "What do you think?"

SOMETHING BETTER

"It's unlike him to just wander off. I wonder if maybe he saw something that interested him."

"You know, he likes animals," Karen said.

"Yeah, maybe a goat or a chicken or something came by, and he followed it."

Jen's attention was drawn to a couple of dogs chasing each other and playing.

She pointed, "Maybe a dog?"

Quinn and Karen looked at each other. They knew their son too well.

"Yeah," Quinn said.

"A dog," Karen added.

"Makes a lot of sense," Jen concurred.

Aaron spoke up, "Okay, following a dog is not that big a deal. The big deal is over there." He pointed to a row of trees a quarter of a mile away. "The river is on the other side of that tree line and that's what we've got to worry about. It's running high from spring melt anyway. Then we had that rain yesterday to add to it. The rapids downstream toward the mill are dangerous. Plus, there's the dam and the falls."

Quinn pictured the ten-foot-high falls pouring over the dam and the grindstone just beyond. His heart began racing. "What are we waiting for? Let's get going."

They started running as best as they could, given Karen's pregnancy, to Shellie's house which was located downstream from the village square. Once they got there, they searched all the way to the river and began methodically combing through the brush along the riverbank. In a matter of moments their worst fears were realized.

"Look at this," Jen pointed. In the mud along the shore were some tracks.

"They're small, like Matt's," Karen said, panting. Adrenaline was pushing her in spite of being pregnant. She grabbed Quinn by the arm. "He must be in the river. Do something!"

He took one look at the rapids downstream and began running. "I'm going to make sure he's not going over the falls by the mill," he called over his shoulder.

"I'm coming with you," Karen yelled.

"We all are," Jen added. She pushed Aaron, "Go back to the village and get more help!"

Quinn was way ahead of everyone, running faster than he ever had in his life, crashing through underbrush lining the shore and slipping in mud. But he kept going fueled by his love for his son. Finally, just upstream from the mill and through a break in the undergrowth he got a clear view of the river. To his horror he saw Matt. "Look," he yelled and pointed to Jen and Karen who were coming up behind him. "He's in the river. Looks like he's hung up on the top of the dam."

Even though he was about two-hundred feet away, Quinn didn't have to think. He dove into the water and swam to save his son. The high-water current carried him along fast, and it took only a minute before he smashed into Matt. He grabbed a hold and held on tight while all around the water rushed past, trying to force them over the dam and into the deadly wheel of the grindstone. The roar of the falls was ear splitting. Quinn tried to talk to Matt, but he was out cold. His lips were blue, and his eyes were closed. It was then he noticed his son was clinging to a little dog. As if for dear life.

Panicking, he turned to scream for help only to see that Jen had swum out to assist in the rescue.

"Here," she yelled, "let me check him." She felt Matt's neck. "He's alive. I can feel a pulse."

"Thank god," Quinn said.

She pointed, "What's with the dog?"

Beside himself with worry, he said, "I have no idea." The force of the river was threatening to dislodge them and carry them all over the dam to certain death, if not by the ten-foot drop over the falls, then by being crushed beneath the wheel of the grindstone. He implored her, "Hurry. We've got to do something."

"We need to get him to shore and warm him up."

Quinn turned and waved to Karen who was standing with Aaron and some of the townspeople. "We've got him," he yelled, but his voice was lost to the booming roar of the river. More villagers were starting to show up. "Let's work him along the top of the dam."

"Good idea."

It took about ten minutes, but they were finally able to get to shore where waiting hands took Matt from them and wrapped him in blankets and administered to him. Quinn noticed the dog stayed close the entire time.

After a few minutes Matt's eyes fluttered open. Then the color began to return to his face. He smiled at his mother, who was on the ground cradling his head in her lap. "Hi, Mom," he said, and hugged her tight. His voice was weak, but his smile said it all. He was going to be okay. Karen hugged him in return, willing warmth from her body into his. Then he asked, "Mom, where's Joey? My dog." And just like that the little dog stepped up, nuzzled in close and began licking Matt's face. He'd been waiting patiently as Matt was being cared for, never having left his side. Matt giggled joyfully and hugged him. "Mom, Joey saved my life."

Karen embraced both her son and the dog, as well as Quinn, who had knelt down and joined them. She had tears of joy in her eyes. "He sure did, honey," she said. "He sure did."

Later that night, Quinn and Karen built a fire outside their small cottage. They had finished dinner and were relaxing, finally starting to come down after the excitement of the day.

Quinn looked at Matt, wrapped in a blanket and cuddling Joey, and said, "Matt, we've got to talk about this. Your mom and I were beside ourselves we were so worried. We almost lost you to that river. Did you learn a lesson today?"

"Yes, Dad, I did. I'm so sorry."

"We escaped from The City, and we've come too far to have something horrible happen now, haven't we?"

"Yes, Dad."

"You really have to learn to me more careful."

They talked some more until Quinn had said all he had

to say. He looked at Karen and she nodded him, silently mouthing, 'Good job.' He risked a smile at her. She smiled back and rested her hand on her stomach, as if silently communicating her familial love for Quinn and Matt and their unborn child. The family was safe and that's what mattered.

As the wood from the fire crackled and the flames lit up their faces, they all sat peacefully with each other and watched the stars come out, happy to be together.

Finally, Matt, who had been quiet, thinking, spoke up and said, "Dad. Mom. I'm really sorry about what happened."

"We know you are, dear," Karen said, reaching over to muss up his curly, red hair. "Just remember what we've told you."

"Yeah, I know. Be careful!"

Karen grinned at him. "Right."

After a few more minutes he, squirmed a little and laughed. Joey was licking him. "Hey, stop that," he grinned and squeezed the little dog tight while kissing his furry forehead. Then he looked at Quinn, "Say, Dad, I was wondering…what do you think? Would it be all right if I kept Joey?"

Quinn grinned at his son. He looked at Karen who nodded her agreement. "Sure," he said. "After all, he saved your life." He reached over and scratched the little dog behind the ears. "Didn't you guy?"

Joey nuzzled Quinn's hand and then went back to cuddling with Matt.

And just like that their little family just got a little bit bigger.

-

SOMETHING BETTER

Chapter Twelve

Joey

"**SO, ARE YOU** excited?" Karen asked, pouring a cup of tea for her and Jen.

"What? About our ceremony and Aaron and me making a commitment to stay together?" Jen joked, tucking a strand of her short-cropped auburn hair behind her ear while taking a sip of the refreshing blend of chamomile and fennel tea Karen was known for.

"No. About catching your first fish yesterday," Karen laughed. "Of course, about your ceremony.

Jen grinned. "Yeah, I am. Aaron's a good guy."

"He is. I'm really happy for you." Karen picked up her four-month-old daughter who'd been playing on the floor with a wooden spoon and kissed the top of her head. "Enya is, too."

Jen set her cup down. "Here. Let me hold her." She took the little girl in her arms and gave her a quick kiss. "Wish me luck, little one. This is a big step for me." She bounced the contented child on her lap as the two friends continued sipping their tea and talking.

"You never thought you'd find someone like Aaron, did you?"

"Not in a million years. Living in The City was such a pain in the ass. Remember when I got mugged that one time? I was happy just to get through one day at work, get home, have something to eat, go to bed and then start all over again."

"I know. Millennium Microbial. What a place to work. It was unbelievable. And Finkelstein. What a jerk."

"No kidding. Not to mention that we didn't have long to live to begin with anyway."

"Yeah. Until we turned forty, if even that long."

"The Lifeline."

"What a weird concept."

"What's so weird about being put to death in the prime of your life just to keep the population under control?"

"Yeah, now when you put it that way, not a thing!"

Both women laughed, something they did often, now that they were living in the quaint community of Nedlaw in the valley of the Willow River.

"So where are Quinn and Matt?" Jen asked, affectionately nuzzling Enya's dark hair. The little girl giggled. "And Joey, of course." Joey was Matt's dog, the brave little terrier who had helped save Matt earlier that spring when he'd fallen into the rain swollen Willow River and nearly been crushed to death under the huge wheel of the grindstone at the mill.

Karen pointed out the window to the foothills rising toward the mountains. It was late summer, and the valley was verdant and green. "The guys took Joey and went on what they called a nature walk." She smiled. "They love it here."

"And they love being together," Jen added.

Karen took Enya in her arms, "Yeah, they do. This has been good for both of them. Just what Quinn wanted."

"And more?" Jen asked pointing to Enya.

"And more," Karen grinned.

Suddenly, the sound of rumbling thunder caught their attention. Karen got up and went to the door of the small cabin and looked out to the mountains to the west. A wall of dark clouds was boiling over them and heading their way. Fast. Lighting was flashing like a strobe light.

"Looks we're in for some wicked weather," she said turning to Jen. "Might put a damper on your ceremony. No pun intended."

Jen laughed. "None taken. We've got the rest of the day until six tonight when it starts."

Karen turned to watch the approaching storm. "I'm getting a little worried about Quinn and Matt, though. They shouldn't be out in this."

"Where'd they go on their nature walk?"

"I think they were heading up Sandy Creek."

"That's on the other side of the river, a couple of miles away. They've got Joey with them, though, so they should be okay. Right?"

"Yeah…" She was going to comment more but instead said, "Oh, shit."

Jen hurried to join her at the door. "What?"

Karen pointed. "Something's wrong."

Jen took one look. "Damn."

Racing out of a grove of trees and crossing a small field on a dead run was Joey. He was all by himself, Quinn, and Matt nowhere in sight. He ran up to where the two women were standing, slid to a halt and began barking frantically. Then he ran a few steps back to where he'd come from, and then ran toward them and then back, barking the entire time. Clearly, he was agitated and trying to get the two of them to follow him.

Jen turned to Karen. "What do you think?"

Karen gave Enya to Jen, grabbed her rain jacket, and started putting it on. "What I think is those two guys are in trouble. You stay with Enya. I'm going to look for them."

"No way. I'm coming with you."

"You can't," Karen pointed. "I need you to stay with her."

"Nope. I'm coming with. End of discussion. I'll tell you what, let's drop her at Shellie's house." Her son and Matt went to school together and were good friends.

"Good idea."

While Jen got ready, Karen bundled up Enya and then knelt down and put a leash on Joey. "Take us to Matt, boy," she said to him. "Help us find Quinn."

SOMETHING BETTER

Joey barked once in acknowledgement and trotted off straining at his leash, Karen and Enya and Jen following behind. They hurried to Shellie's cottage first.

"I'll be glad to take Enya," she said, her face showing her concern after Karen told her what was happening. "I'll get a hold of Aaron and we'll get some help organized."

Karen hugged Shellie. "Thank you so much." She kissed Enya, handed her over to Shellie and said to Jen, "Let's go!"

Fifteen minutes later, Joey was leading them across the wooden footbridge that spanned the Willow River. Halfway across, the skies opened up and it began to rain. A downpour was more like it, one like they'd never seen before. Thunder boomed, lightning flashed all around them, and Quinn and Matt were out in it. Karen's heart was pounding in her chest. Where were they?

After crossing the bridge, the two women turned to their left and began sprinting as fast as they could toward Sandy Creek with Joey on his leash pulling them along. Then, as if to make matters worse, the rain began increasing in intensity. In moments they were drenched.

Two miles away in the bottom of a steep gully, Matt cradled his father's head in his lap. "Dad! Dad, can you hear me?" Blood was running from a gash in Quinn's forehead into his eyes and Matt was struggling to wipe it away, fighting back tears. He had just turned six years old and was getting to be a 'Big boy,' as he thought of himself, but other than keeping the blood out of his dad's eyes, he didn't know what else he should do. One thing he did know instinctively, though, was that he had to be strong.

Quinn groaned and blinked a few times, starting to come around. "W…Wa…What happened?"

"You slipped and fell down the hill, Dad," Matt said, wiping more blood away. "I…I think you cut yourself."

As Quinn slowly moved his head back and forth, clearing his vision, the events earlier in the day started coming back to him. Yeah, that's right, he had fallen. He and Matt had decided to take a hike before Jen and Aaron's ceremony, mainly to get out of the way while the final preparations were being made. They crossed the Willow River and followed it until they met up with Sandy Creek, a narrow tributary that flowed from the glaciers high in the mountains. At Matt's urging they'd followed the creek into the foothills looking for wildflowers and watching for wildlife.

When Quinn had seen a huge bird soaring above them, he'd pointed it out to Matt. "Look. Look at the big raptor. It's an eagle. A golden eagle."

Matt looked up, spied the bird and said, "That's so cool, Dad."

When he had stepped back to give Matt more room to see, Quinn slipped on some loose gravel, lost his footing, and fell off the trail, tumbling down a steep slope, rolling over and over before finally coming to rest at the bottom of a gully. He might have been all right except that he'd cracked his head on a boulder on the way down and smashed his face into the trunk of a dead pine tree once he'd come to rest at the bottom. Then he'd passed out, only coming around when he recognized Matt's voice.

"I'm starting to feel a little better," he said. Quinn knew he had to try to ignore the pain he was in so he could take care of his son. "I'm going to try to…oh, oh." He was trying to sit up when the world started spinning around and around making him so dizzy, he almost got sick to his stomach. "I think I'd better keep lying down."

Matt helped his father lay back and then leaned over him and gently brushed the hair out of eyes. And some more blood. "Dad, you just rest." He took the cork out of an earthenware water container and held it to his father's lips. "Here. Drink some of this. You'll feel better."

Quinn drank thirstily. "Thanks. I needed that. You're a good helper." Then he looked around. "Hey, where's Joey?"

"He was worried about you. I could tell. Like I was. So, told him to run home to Mom and bring help."

Quinn had trouble believing a dog could be that smart, but who was he to argue? Right now, injured like he was and not able to help himself, anything was better than nothing. "You think he understood you?"

"Oh, yeah, Dad. Joey's real smart."

A crack of lightning overhead made them both flinch. It was followed by booming thunder like someone pounding on a kettle drum. Fast moving black clouds began rolling over the nearby mountains, and in a matter of moments rain drops the size of small stones started hitting the ground. And them. Splat. Splat. Splat.

With his dad's head still cradled in his lap, Matt bent over him to use his little body to offer protection from the sudden downpour. It didn't help. In a minute they were both drenched by the cold rain. Then it started to hail. Quinn began shivering and so did Matt. They held on to each other but the cold cut through them like a knife. They were trapped and unable to escape and could do nothing now but hope that by some miracle Joey could find help and bring people back to rescue them. Until then all they had was each other.

Thunder shook the ground and lightning lit up the sky. Rain fell in sheets whipped by gusting winds, pelting Karen and Jen in their faces like steel pellets. Neither woman had ever seen such a storm. To make matters worse, pea sized hail began falling, battering them on their hunched shoulders and coating the ground.

Karen pointed up Sandy Creek toward the foothills and yelled to Jen above the wind, "Quinn said they were heading that way." She wiped the rain from her eyes. Some tears, too. "I'm worried. It's dangerous for them to be out in this storm."

Just as she spoke Joey broke from the leash and took off at a dead run along the side of the creek, splashing through puddles and kicking up tiny bits of gravel and hail.

Jen didn't hesitate. "Let's go!" she yelled.

The two of them took off at a sprint after the little dog. A cacophony of thunder was booming all around them, drowning out the thumping of their beating hearts. It was tough going, fighting their way up hill. The terrain was rocky and the loose gravel and stones under foot made walking hard on a good day and even more treacherous now that they were wet. Brown, murky runoff flooded toward them from further up in the hills and with every passing minute the storm seemed to intensify as the howling wind buffeted them with horizontally driven rain. At least the hail had quit.

SOMETHING BETTER

Joey ran ahead, stopped, and ran back to them and ran ahead again, encouraging them to go faster. Sometimes he ran out of their vision but always returned. He gave the women hope.

Karen was beside herself with worry. She and Quinn and Matt had gone through too much for something horrible to occur that would put an end it all. She couldn't let that happen.

As if reading her friend's thoughts, Jen yelled above the wind, "Don't worry, we'll find them."

Karen slowed to catch her breath. "I just don't know where they could be. Quinn mentioned coming up the creek, but he didn't say how far."

Jen wiped water from her face, trying to see ahead, but it was impossible. Rain was pouring down so hard it was like they were standing under a waterfall. Hail started falling again and was pounding them, bouncing off the ground like popping corn. Their range of vision was only about fifty feet.

Suddenly, up ahead they heard the frantic barking of Joey. Jen pulled Karen along, "Let's hurry. Joey's up there. He must be trying to tell us something."

Karen mustered all of her strength and off they ran toward Joey, hoping they weren't too late.

When Joey saw Karen and Jen coming toward him, he leaped into the gully and slid down to Matt and Quinn. The women ran to the edge and looked. About thirty feet below them, Karen saw Matt bent over his dad but neither of them was moving. Joey was at their side, desperately barking and licking at Matt, then nuzzling Quinn, then back to licking Matt.

Quickly, Karen went over the edge and slid down the wet slope, taking in the scene the instant she was at the bottom. Quinn had a gash on his forehead with blood seeping out of it mingling with rainwater. There was also a scrape on the back of his head. Matt appeared uninjured but was very cold. He shivered when she picked him up. "Mom's here, honey," she said, hugging him before handing over him to Jen who had slid down right behind her. "He's really cold, but other than that I think he's okay. Check him out and see what you think."

"I'm on it." Jen and Matt were close friends. She cradled him to her chest for a moment before laying him down to check his vital signs, bending over him to keep the rain off. Thankfully, the hail had stopped, hopefully for good. "Hey there, guy," she spoke softly trying to be calm. "I'm here. You're safe now. How are you feeling?"

Matt opened his eyes to a blurry world. He turned toward where the voice was coming from as his vision began to clear. When he recognized Jen, his face lit up. "Aunt Jen," he grinned, and threw his arms around her neck hugging her. "Boy am I ever glad to see you." He pointed. "Is Dad, okay?"

Jen looked at Karen who was administering to her husband and asked, "Karen, how is he?"

Karen had ripped a piece of fabric from her shirt and had used it to clean the wound on Quinn's forehead. She was now working on the one on the back of his head. "The scrapes aren't too deep. I think he's going to be okay."

When he heard their voices, Quinn began to regain

consciousness and tried to sit up. "I'm okay. Ow!" He stiffly lay again. "Well, maybe not. My head…it really hurts."

Karen turned to Jen. "He might have a concussion. We'll have to be careful with him." To Quinn she said, "You just rest for a little bit." She picked up a nearby water container and opened it, holding the rim to Quinn's lips. "Here you go. Drink this." Quinn gratefully did.

It took over an hour to get Quinn and Matt up out of the gully and then down from the hills toward the village. On the way they met Aaron and a search party sent out by Shellie. By the time they got to Quinn and Karen's cabin everyone was soaking wet and bone cold.

Jen and Aaron helped Karen start a fire and soon the little cabin was nice and warm and toasty. They all put on dry clothes, even Jen and Aaron, who borrowed some of Jen's and Quinn's. Matt and Quinn sat by the fire with Enya. Quinn's head was wrapped in a fresh bandage that was originally a cotton shirt of his. He had a headache but both Karen and Jen agreed that he didn't have a concussion, just a couple of bad scrapes.

Aaron heated some potato and vegetable stew while Jen cut up thick slices of Karen's bread in preparation of a warm and filling meal. Karen busied herself setting the table, trying not to berate Quinn. But finally, she couldn't help it.

"Quinn, I can't believe you were so clumsy out there. You've got to be more careful."

"I know. I'm sorry." And he was. "I'll be more conscientious next time."

Matt chimed in, "When can we go back, Dad? I want to

see that eagle again."

"When your mother says it's okay," Quinn said.

He looked at Karen, who winked and said, "You've got that right, buddy." Then she smacked her forehead. "Wait a minute. What about the ceremony?" She turned to Jen. "I'm so sorry. I forgot all about it."

Jen smiled at her. "That's okay. Me and Aaron have been talking. We're just happy this all worked out as well as it did. We're going to postpone it until later. That'll be the best thing to do. Plus..." she paused as the little cottage shook with a loud crack of lightning exploding nearby. "This is a pretty wicked storm."

"You sure?" Karen asked.

Jen looked at Aaron who nodded and smiled back at her. She said, "Yep. It's all good."

Joey stood up from his spot next to Matt by the fire, yawned and stretched before laying down again. Matt hugged the little terrier and said, "I'm so happy I have Joey. I think he saved us."

Quinn looked at Karen who looked at Jen who looked at Aaron. Everyone was smiling and nodding their heads in the affirmative. Quinn grinned and looked back to his son and said, "You know what, I think you're right. Joey's a real member of the family now."

Close by the fire the little terrier stayed sleeping, but wagged his tail slowly, as if heard what was being said about him. And he agreed with every word.

-

SOMETHING BETTER

Chapter Thirteen

The Drone

BUCK BENSON, FORMER security squad leader for the Regional Food Storage Facility, had never gotten over that fiasco from just over a year ago. His boss wouldn't let him forget it either.

"You know, Buck," general Rawlings told while they were having drinks at the Last Outpost, a sleazy bar near where they worked, "Commander Langer from the World Order Security Police wanted me to fire you."

Buck nodded his head glumly. "Yeah, I figured he would."

"I saved your ass."

"Yeah," Buck responded morosely. "Now I get to work doing roving security like that idiot Anderson used to do."

Anderson had been the security shift leader on that infamous night last year and had been demoted by Rawlings to a computer tech in the IT room. Benson had taken over Anderson's job, a demotion from security squad leader he didn't appreciate. "Thanks a bunch." He slammed down his Sortabeer and signaled for another. Then he took a small container from his pocket and popped a pill.

"At least you've still got a job," Rawlings reminded him, then pointed to the pills and said, "Better go easy on those bad boys. Don't want to get drunk. Big day tomorrow."

"You mean with that nut-case Langer coming by to read us the riot act? Big friggin' deal."

Fearful someone would overhear, Rawlings quickly glanced over his shoulder. When he was convinced no one was paying them any attention he whispered, "Look, I know what you mean. Just cool it, okay?"

Buck snorted derisively. He made a move to put his container away, but Rawlings stopped him. "Wait. Give me one of those." Buck handed over one of his "relaxer" pills as he called them to his boss. Then he took another for himself while waiting for his drink to arrive. They both knew tomorrow was going to be a long day. There was talk of going after the escapees that had been slipping past the Food Storage security team the last year, a number that seemed to grow larger with every month. If that happened chances were excellent the ending could get messy and both of them knew it. When Buck's drink arrived the men didn't notice, they just sat staring into space and contemplating the future. It didn't look pretty at all.

After a rainy week, the day of Jen's commitment ceremony

dawned clear under a cloudless sky.

"Look at the sunrise!" she exclaimed to her friend Karen who had come over to her quaint cottage early to help with final preparations.

"Looks great," Karen said with hardly a glance. Known for her scrumptious dark brown whole wheat and honey bread, she was trying her hand at making blue berry muffins and having a hard time of it. She slammed her wooden spoon down on the table with an accompanying, "Damn!" and said, "I think I'll take a break." She poured a cup of chamomile and fennel tea and joined her friend looking out the window.

Jen pointed, "See."

The sun's rays were racing across the valley floor as it rose over the mountains to the east. The snow was gleaming white on the tops of the peaks reflecting the golden dawn light that was bringing with it the promise of a lovely late summer day. Songbirds were greeting the sun with jubilant singing and there was a pine scented freshness in the air from the ever-green forests doting the nearby hillsides. In the distance the rushing rapids of the Willow River could just barely be heard as it tumbled over its rocky streambed on its way through the valley.

Jen had opened the window and calico curtains wafted in a light breeze. Karen took a deep breath of the fresh sage tinted air as she sipped her tea and immediately began to calm down. "That's better," she said. "Much better," she smiled at Jen. Then, after gazing at the sunrise for a minute, she sighed and said, "I do love it here."

"You don't mind not having a lot of the conveniences that we had back in The City?"

"Like running water?"

Jen laughed. "Yeah, it did take a while to get used to pumping our own. And making most of our own food. But I like it. It's making me feel independent." She flexed her muscle. "Not to mention stronger."

Karen laughed. "It's just an adjustment, that's all. I don't mind. I'm learning new skills, and Quinn and Matt and Enya are happy. Life is good."

"Speaking of Quinn, where is he? He's coming to the ceremony, right?"

"Wouldn't miss it. He and the kids are working in our garden digging out another plot for next year."

"Joey helping?"

"Of course. After helping to save Matt's life at the mill last spring and Quinn's life in the gully last week, Joey's a bonified member of the family now."

"Don't let it go to his head."

"No way. He may be smart, but he's humble. You can just tell."

Jen looked at Karen and grinned, joking, "Sounds like you've thought about this a lot."

"I guess I have." She laughed. Then she turned to the worktable where the dough was waiting. "Better get back to these muffins."

Jen said, "I'll help. We've got time yet. The ceremony's not until high sun."

"You excited?"

"Yeah, I am. Aaron and I get along well. We make a good

team."

Karen laughed. "Sounds romantic."

Jen laughed with her. "You know what I mean."

Karen did. The success of her relationship with Quinn was their willingness to forgo personal idiosyncrasies for the good of their family, relying on each other's strengths to form a strong family unit. They'd been together for seven years and were still learning about each other.

Jen interrupted Karen's thoughts, "You know, I think we should hold the ceremony outside instead of in the meeting hall. It's just so nice out!"

Karen looked up from kneading the muffin dough and out the window. The late summer day was indeed glorious. "Go for it. It's a beautiful day for a gathering."

"We'll hold it right outside the meeting house."

Karen wiped her hands on her apron and joined her friend, both of them looking outside. "It's your day, and your idea sounds perfect."

"Let's do it, then," Jen said, and suddenly broke into a spontaneous set of dance moves and concentric twirls around the kitchen. Breathlessly, she smiled, when she was finished, "You know, I've never been happier."

"I can see that," Karen grinned at her. "Me, neither."

Buck Benson shifted uncomfortably in the hard-plastic chair, not at all happy with what Commander Langer was saying.

"In summary, you've all been screwing up. People in ones and twos and small groups have been escaping The City as long as I can remember and I'm sick of it. It's got to stop!"

The overweight man stopped his tirade and wiped his massive brow with a stained handkerchief. Buck leaned over to Rawlings who was sitting at attention, and whispered, "Is this guy for real? Who cares if a few people leave The City? It means more of everything for us, right? You know that food is in short supply."

"Langer's a jerk. He's ego is so huge it won't let him live with the fact that he can't control everyone."

"I hate him."

"Shh. Don't let anyone hear you," Rawlings put his finger to his lips and looked around. Fortunately, the one-hundred or so people in the meeting hall were paying rapt attention to the head of the World Order Security Police.

He continued, his voice shaking with rage, "I'm telling my men from now on to set their laser guns to 'kill' and blast anyone trying to escape to kingdom come. They're under strict orders to not take any prisoners." He pointed at general Rawlings, who, Buck noticed, immediately had sweat droplets bead up on his face. "And I want you, Rawlings, to do the same with your men. Too many people are getting through the fence surrounding your facility, not to mention those three scientists and that kid last year. That still pisses me off!" He slammed his fist on the podium causing the microphone to emit a high-pitched screaming feedback that forced all those present to cover their ears. He jabbed his finger at Rawlings, causing him to flinch, "You got that?"

"Yes…" he said, clearing his throat. "Yes, sir," he barked. "Understood. Sir."

SOMETHING BETTER

Buck glanced at his boss as Langer continued his ranting diatribe against the world and specifically how incompetently The City was being run. General Rawlings was visibly shaken that the Regional Food Storage Facility he was in charge of had come under such microscopic scrutiny. Buck felt for him. Rawlings wasn't a bad sort, but Langer was an entirely different beast. In Buck's mind, the guy was a psychopath. You never knew what he was going to do or come up with to have others do for him.

Buck gave Rawlings the universal 'thumbs up' sign, letting him know he was on his side. Rawlings returned it before taking a drink of bottled water. Then he leaned over and said, "I'm going need your help. I'm going to give you your old job back. No more roving security for you. I want you to be in charge of the patrols like before. You'll be Security Squad Leader again." He looked Buck right in the eye. "And this time don't screw up!"

Buck gulped. Shit. This wasn't what he wanted. He liked the anonymity of being a roving security guard. "Are you sure, sir? I really don't mind what I'm doing now."

"I know, but Langer sent me a message earlier today and asked for you specifically. Said that it was time to see if you'd learned your lesson."

"Great," Buck said, sarcastically. "Just great."

"Oh, and one other thing," Rawlings leaned closer. Buck could feel the heart emanating from the general's body, and he wondered how much of it was fear. "He wants us to take the lead on surveillance in this location."

"What's that entail?"

"Among other things, he wants us to send out our drone

and comb the area looking for escapees."

"Really?" Buck was suddenly enthusiastic. He liked playing with gadgets and the drone was one of the best, much better than the video games he was addicted to.

"Yeah. Starting today."

"That's fantastic. Where are we going to concentrate?

"I'm thinking well scour the desert west of here and see what there is to see. If we don't find anything, we'll send it into the mountains."

Buck was excited. This would be something new, and a chance to do something different for a change. Suddenly, he was looking forward to it. "Sounds great, sir."

"I want you to pilot the drone."

"You mean command the software, right?"

"Of course. You'll be safe in the control room the whole time."

Having a hard time keeping his growing excitement under control, Buck managed a subdued, "Sounds good, sir." Inwardly, though, he was thrilled. Maybe this new assignment would be his chance to finally prove himself after letting those three scientists and kid escape. He hoped so.

They turned their attention to Commander Langer who was now talking about how great The City was going to be in five years. Both Buck and Rawlings were thinking the same thing, *God, would this guy never shut up?*

Quinn placed a big bowl of blackberries on the food-laden table set up in front of Aaron and Jen, gave them each a good luck hug and went back to join his family. All the villagers had congregated on the front yard of the meeting house across the street from the village green, a park that was a gathering place for the four-hundred or so citizens of Nedlaw.

Matt tapped his dad on the shoulder and asked, "Why are we here again?"

Quinn smiled, "It's for Jen and Aaron's special ceremony. They're going to make a commitment to be with each other for the rest of their life."

"The rest of their life?" Matt's eyes grew wide. "That's a long time!"

Quinn grinned and looked at Karen who was holding four-month-old Enya. "If you love someone enough it's actually quite short."

Matt made a face. "Yuck." Then he looked around, hoping to spy Gary his best friend from school. Next to him, Joey, his feisty little terrier, sat quietly taking it all in. The day had warmed up and most of the villagers were wearing light cotton, summer clothes. The harvest would begin next month, and Quinn was already busy cutting firewood to augment the solar collectors on their cabin. It was to be their second winter and he knew they had to be prepared for cold weather and long days of snow-bound isolation.

His thoughts of upcoming chores to be completed were interrupted when Aaron said, "Okay, everyone, we might as well begin."

"First of all, welcome," Jen spread her arms wide. "We're glad so many of our friends could join us on this beautiful day."

Quinn listened as Aaron and Jen talked in simple terms about their love and commitment for each other and then finished by both of them saying, "So let us celebrate not only our life together, but our life together with you, our cherished friends and our wonderful village."

There was good natured laughter and applause. A fiddle, guitar and wooden flute began playing a lively reel and people moved to the front and started dancing. Quinn reached over and gave Karen and Enya a hug. "That was nice," he said.

"Yes, it was," Karen smiled. Then a worried frown crossed her face, "Wait a minute. Where's Matt?"

Heart's racing, they both looked quickly around, panicking that he'd run off like last spring and fallen in the river and nearly drowned. After a moment, though, they were able to sigh with relief. He was with his friend Gary. They had wandered away from the crowd and were pointing to the sky. Quinn walked over to find out what was going on. "Hey there, guys. What're you looking at?"

"Look, Dad." Matt pointed to a small object circling over the valley about one-hundred yards off the ground. "Is that a bird? An eagle?"

Quinn squinted against the sun and took a look. Then a closer look. His heart leaped into this throat as knelt down and pulled Matt to him. He looked him in the eyes and said, "Go to your mom. Hurry. Gary, you run to your mom, too."

As the boys sped off, Quinn ran up to Aaron who was dancing with Jen. "Aaron, we've got trouble," he said, pointing to the sky.

SOMETHING BETTER

Aaron smiled quickly faded, "What?"

"Look," Quinn said.

Aaron quickly focused on the object. "Damn," he swore, "A drone. Must be from The City."

After being in the village for just over a year, it was the first drone Quinn had ever seen. In fact, he'd never really thought about even seeing one, so he was a little rattled, "What are we going to do?"

"I've got this," Aaron said. "Go wait with Karen. I'll join you in a minute." Then, he quickly took charge. "Okay, everyone," he pointed to the sky, "there's drone in the area. Don't panic, but hurry and get out of sight. Those of you that can make it to your homes, please do so." He and Jen began to usher people away from the front yard of the meeting house, repeating again, "Okay, a drone is in the area. Get to your homes. Get into hiding." As the villagers hurried away and everything seemed under control for the moment, they ran to where Quinn and Karen were waiting along with Matt and Enya and Joey. Aaron spoke urgently to Jen, "Okay. We talked about this. Remember?"

"Yep, I do," she said, and handed Enya to Quinn. "Take Matt and Enya back to the cottage and stay put." She saw the questioning look in his eye and said, "Don't worry. We've planned for this." When Quinn hesitated, Karen pushed him, "I'll tell you about it later. Go. Now!"

He went, carrying Enya as he began running with Matt and Joey. He couldn't help but notice the drone circling closer and closer. He glanced over his shoulder and saw Karen running toward the river with Jen and Aaron. Where were they going?

He put his worry aside. If there was one thing he knew, it was that Karen was the most level-headed person he'd ever met, just the kind of person who was needed in a situation like this.

"Come on, Matt. Let's get home," he said taking his son's hand and running even faster, Joey right beside them. Above them, the drone circled ever closer, watching their every move.

SOMETHING BETTER

Chapter Fourteen

Nerves of Steel

BUCK BENSON HAD never had so much fun at his job. Being Security Squad Leader was one thing, but, frankly, keeping watch over the perimeter of the Regional Food Storage Facility and looking out for escapees was kind of boring. But this, he shifted in his chair as well as making a shift in the position of the drone he was flying, this was fun.

The next moment, however, that good time exploded like a fragmentation bomb when his boss general Rawlings hurried into the surveillance room with Commander Langer following in lockstep right behind.

Immediately, Buck put the drone on autopilot, stood up, snapped to attention, and saluted both men, something he wouldn't have had to do if it were just Rawlings. After all, they were almost friends. But Langer was a force to be reckoned with, a larger-than-life man who delighted in making everyone around him uncomfortable, especially Benson and Rawlings, so it was best to play along and try not to antagonize him.

In Buck's opinion the guy was a raving lunatic. But he was also the high-ranking Head of Security for the World Order Security Police for the City which included the Region Food Storage Facility. He had it in for the two of them because occasionally people escaped through the fence surrounding the facility, something that drove Langer absolutely insane. Which, truth be told, was something Buck and Rawlings didn't mind seeing.

Still, the commander was the ultimate person overseeing what Rawlings, and, by association, Benson, did on the job, and he wasn't happy with either of them, a dislike going all the back to last year when three young scientists and a small boy had made it through the fence and into the desert. Since then, Langer had vowed revenge, both on anyone escaping, as well as on Rawlings and Benson. That being the case, it wasn't at all surprising to Buck that Langer had made this unannounced appearance for an inspection to check up on them.

"How's surveillance with the drone going, Benson?" Rawlings asked, trying to sound official.

Buck tried his best to make Rawlings look good to Langer.

"Great, sir." He sat down and took the drone off autopilot. "Take a look at this."

Motioning for Rawlings and Langer to stand behind him, he pointed at the large monitor. "See that?" The drone's camera was showing real-time video that was crystal-clear.

SOMETHING BETTER

"My god," Rawlings exclaimed. "What is that?"

The video was showing a bleak landscape and a more foreboding country could not be imagined. It was a rocky, hilly wasteland devoid of vegetation. The only moving things were dust devils swirling across the desert floor. "It's the desert west of here, sir. I refer to it as No Man's Land. Pretty bad, isn't it?"

"I've heard rumors," Rawlings answered, with a touch awe in his voice. "I've never seen anything more desolate in my life."

"No kidding. The drone's been out for over a week and sending back images the entire time. It's nothing, but nothing out there," Buck said, smiling at his joke. He glanced at Rawlings who made a quick 'cut it' slashing motion across his throat. With Langer in the room, it was not a time to be anything other than strictly professional. Buck got the message and turned back to the monitor.

After the three of them silently watched the video feed for a minute (which was a minute of watching basically nothing), Buck could sense Langer was getting restless, so he decided to show off a little. He brought the drone down close to the ground. "See that?" He glanced at Rawlings who along with Langer was now looking at the big monitor more closely. Rawlings nodded imperceptibly, approving of Buck's decision to show Langer what he could do. "I just found them today. Those are wild dogs."

"Interesting," Rawlings stated his approval. "I've heard they were out there."

"There are. This is the first pack I've gotten a close look at."

Langer, who had been silent up until then and getting increasingly bored was suddenly intrigued. "Show me how the laser works."

"Sir?"

"The laser, Benson, you idiot. Show me how it works."

"I don't understand, sir. It works fine. Look." He pushed a button and instantly a rock exploded and turned to dust. "See."

Langer wasn't impressed. "Take out something living, you moron." He pointed, "Like one of those dogs."

"What?" Buck exclaimed. "No, sir. Not one of the dogs. Wasn't the rock good enough?" He glanced at Rawlings who shrugged his shoulders as if to say, 'What can you do?' and kept his mouth shut. It wouldn't do to contradict Langer. The guy was a powerful man who could easily snap his fingers and have one or both of them killed at a moment's notice. Or do it himself, which was an equally disturbing thought.

Langer gave Buck a steely look. "What's wrong, Benson, not man enough?" He raised his voice into a falsetto range, "You a little girly girl?" He sang in a sing-song way and stared haughtily at his subordinate, challenging him to perform on command.

Buck felt the blood rush to his face. He didn't want to kill anything but neither did he want to look like a coward in front of the head of the World Order Security Police.

"Okay, sir," he said, trying, but failing miserably, he knew, to sound enthusiastic. "Whatever you say, sir."

He aimed the drone's laser in the vicinity of the sleeping pack. The coordinates for them were immediately calculated.

"I'm waiting," Langer said rubbing his hands together in a perverted show of anticipation. Buck glanced at Rawlings who again looked away, having as tough time as he was stomaching the demented and unnecessary order. Next to them Langer grinned and chuckled like a deranged clown. He was conscious of the two men's feelings of revulsion and was enjoying every moment of making them feel ill at ease.

Buck sighed and wiped his perspiring brow. "Okay. Here goes." He pushed a button and one of the dogs exploded in a mass of blood and guts. The others ran off, much to Buck's relief.

"Yea!" Langer punched a triumphant arm into the air. "Excellent!" He jabbed a finger in Buck's face. "You find anybody out there, Benson, make sure to do that to them." Langer smiled a rare smile which revealed tiny yellow teeth. "On second thought, let me know if you find any humans and I'll be right over. I want to be here when you blast them to kingdom come."

With Langer's sobering comment hanging in the air, Buck and Rawlings looked at each other and rolled their eyes, a risky move, but they couldn't help it. In their opinion, to say Langer was unhinged was putting it mildly. More to the point he was a raving psychopath who only cared about himself and his career. Any shred of human feelings and emotions were long gone. Having him as their boss was bad enough, having to be in the same room with him was unbearable.

Glumly, Buck replied, "Yes, sir." He turned to Rawlings and said, "That's it, sir. That's all I've got to show you."

Very good, Benson," Rawlings said. Then, realizing Buck

felt bad about the dog, he quickly ushered Langer to the door. "Let's go down the hall, Commander, I want to show you our new video system for monitoring the perimeter of the facility."

"Lead on," Langer said, but before they took a step, he grabbed Rawlings by the shoulder and spun him around, so they were eye to eye. "And, Rawlings," he said, sneering at him, "this better be good."

"Yes…Yes, sir," Rawlings stammered.

Buck saw sweat bead up on his bosses' forehead and then watched as the two men turned and walked away. He sighed. He didn't envy Rawlings one bit for having to show Langer around the facility. A thankless job, in his opinion, one you couldn't pay him enough to do.

With their footsteps echoing down the hall, Buck turned to his monitoring station and starred at the screen, not really paying much attention to the drone as it made its way into the mountains. He couldn't shake the image of the exploding wild dog from in his brain, and he was trying his hardest not to think about taking it a step further and doing the same thing to innocent human beings. So far, he'd been lucky because he hadn't found any escapees and he was glad. Picturing himself doing to real live people what Langer had made him do to the wild dog made him just about want to puke. He didn't have to think twice, with Langer now on his case all the fun had gone out of his new job.

Turning his attention to the monitor, Buck made himself focus on the task at hand. He flew the drone over the mountains and took a moment to marvel at the breath-taking scenery: the pine forests, clear rushing streams and snow-covered peaks. He'd never seen anything like it before in his life. He could almost smell the fresh air, imagining it to be much different from the stale polluted stuff people were forced to breathe in The City unless they used their oxygen masks. He was almost envious of the escapees.

But he had a job to do, so when he flew the drone into a valley with a river in it and then came upon an unexpected village, he was surprised as well as anxious. He could see people scurrying in all directions, trying to escape and hide. He almost felt sorry for them. "Hmm," he said out loud to no one but himself, remembering his orders and especially Langer's words about blasting people to kingdom come. He zeroed in on a man carrying a small child holding the hand of a young boy with a dog running alongside. "He looks good. I'll take him out. Maybe get those two kids and the dog, too. Yeah, that's an idea. Four for the price of one."

Suddenly, he paused and berated himself, thinking, *Wait a minute! What's happening to me? What am I doing? These are innocent people!"* And he almost convinced himself right then and there how wrong it was to do what he was about to do. Almost, but he couldn't. No, he had Rawlings and Langer to contend with. Plus, he had his orders, and there was nothing he could do about that. He got ready to follow through on them.

Earlier, when Matt spied the drone and pointed it out to his dad, Quinn had run to Aaron and the alarm had been raised. In an instant, the villagers responded by hurrying to their homes and doing their best to get out of sight. Quinn did the same and began running with Matt and Enya and Joey back to their cabin.

Karen and Jen, on the other hand, were an exception. They had gone with Aaron to a small building on the outskirts of the village on the other side of the Willow River.

When they stepped inside, Aaron picked up an old pair of binoculars and said to the two women, "Okay, like we've practiced, you two take over. I'll watch for more drones."

"I'll monitor the energy level," Jen said, sitting down at a computer counsel.

Karen sat down next to her at her own counsel. She took a moment to center herself by closing her eyes and controlling her breathing. When felt herself get into what she called 'The Zone' she deftly touched a few keys. In a moment, a view of the valley appeared on her screen. A few more adjustments and she said, "Okay, I'm all set. The coordinates have been calculated."

Buck lined up the laser sight that appeared on his screen. The drone's computer had automatically calculated everything that was necessary to score a direct hit on the man. *Just like a video game*, he thought. When he was confident everything was all set, he made a quick call to Rawlings. "Hello, sir. Is Commander Langer still with you? I think I've something here he'll enjoy."

"What is it, Benson?" Rawlings barked. "I'm pretty busy here."

Langer must be still with him. "Sorry to bother you, sir, but I've got some people in my sights. I thought Langer would like to come and watch me blast them."

The response was quick and decisive, "We're just down

the hall. I'll…We'll be right there."

Less than a minute later the two men hurried into the control room. "What's going on?" Rawlings asked.

"Just this, sir." Buck pointed at the monitor. The drone was still hovering over the fleeing man and his kids and dog.

Rawlings leaned in and took a good look before tuning to Langer, "Commander, check this out. It's guy and a baby and a kid and a dog."

Langer pushed Rawlings aside in his excitement. He was so close that Buck could sniff his body odor, a smell reminiscent of rotting garbage. He fought back a gag reflex and shifted in his chair ever so slightly away from the putrid smelling man.

Langer grinned, "What are you waiting for, Benson, you idiot. Blast 'em! Blast 'em to kingdom come!"

"Aye, aye, sir," Buck said, not knowing why he spoke those exact words, words he'd never spoken before in his life. Maybe nerves. He really didn't want to kill anyone. He looked once more. These were just innocent people. However, with his two bosses standing right behind him, Buck didn't have a choice. He took a deep breath, exhaled, and said, "Okay, here we go."

Jen checked her monitor. The energy level was still good. She turned to Karen and asked, "Are you ready?"

"I'm more than ready," she said. "We can't let The City get in here to our peaceful valley and ruin our way of life. We've come too far to give it up."

Jen smiled, "That's the spirit. I told Aaron we could depend on you."

Aaron turned from his binoculars and said to Karen, "You're right about The City. I can tell by the drone's markings that's where it's from. Looks like the Regional Food Storage Facility."

Jen glanced at Aaron, "That's where the fence was where we escaped. What do you suppose it's doing out here?"

"Probably on a fact-finding mission." Aaron put his binoculars up and was quiet for a moment. "You know, this can't be good. It looks like the drone has locked onto a target."

He turned to Karen. "You ready to take it out?"

"More than ready." Karen nodded with a determination in her eyes that was coursing through her entire body. She was coiled like a snake ready to strike.

In the next moment Karen turned to her monitor and checked her calculations and the coordinates one more time. Everything looked perfect. She glanced to friend, "You ready Jen?"

"Yep. The laser is powered up."

"Aaron?"

"All set."

"Okay," Karen said. "Me, too." She raised her hand above the keyboard, hesitated but a micro-second and then pushed a button. "Say good-bye to Mr. Drone."

Just as Buck was about to fire the laser, something unexpected happened. The screen went blank. He quickly checked his readings. There was nothing. The drone was gone, like it had vanished into thin air. Buck's only thought was, *Oh, oh. This can't be good.*

He glanced at Rawlings who stared back at him eyes wide, waiting, Benson just knew, for Langer to explode. It didn't take long, and when he exploded, he erupted like a volcano spewing hot, molten lava a mile into the air, which some might have found a pretty sight, but in the case of Langer, and, especially for Rawlings and Benson, it wasn't a pretty sight. Not at all.

When the drone disintegrated, the cheers from the little building could probably have been heard all the way back in the village, if anyone was still around. But the village was empty with most everybody safely hidden away in their homes. In the end, that was good, because at least Karen and Jen and Aaron saw what had happened, and they had the story to tell when they gathered everyone together later that afternoon.

"Karen blasted that drone right out of the sky," Aaron said to the villagers as they all congregated in the village green under a warm, sunny sky. His smile seemed to be a mile wide, "It was beautiful."

Jen chimed in, "It was so exciting. First you saw it, then you didn't. Boom!" she pantomimed an explosion, much to the delight of the crowd.

"It was right above us when it exploded," Quinn told everyone who would listen, and everyone did. "They saved our lives."

For the next hour or so, Karen smiled and nodded and

accepted the villager's heartfelt congratulations until she finally pulled Quinn aside and said, "I'm exhausted. Can we go home?"

He hugged her. "Good idea." They said their good-byes and the little family slowly made their way through the village, across a field and down a meandering path to a clearing in an aspen forest where their snug cabin was located. It had been a long day and it felt good to be home.

Later that night the little family was outside siting around a crackling campfire. Jen and Aaron had joined them and were snuggled together sipping some dandelion wine Aaron had made. Next to them Matt was dozing holding Joey in his arms. Quinn was sitting next to Karen who was cradling Enya.

Quinn put his arm around his wife and nuzzled their daughter before saying to Karen, "I'm so happy things turned out the way they did, but I can't believe you didn't tell me that Aaron had recruited you." He gave her a playful jab. "For a whole year! You keep secrets well.'"

Karen gave him a quick kiss and said, "I just didn't want you to worry." She shifted Enya and nodded toward Matt, who was still asleep with Joey's head in his lap, oblivious to the conversation going on around him. "I know how much you tend to do that."

Quinn laughed, "Yeah, you're probably right."

Jen said, "You know what a good scientist Karen was back in the City? Working for Millennium Microbial?"

Quinn nodded and winked at Karen as he leaned over and tossed another log on the fire. Sparks rose briefly before burning out. "Working on that project to help extend the world's food supplies? You were the best. Even if that jerk you worked for didn't get it."

"Finkelstein?" Karen said. "Yeah, good riddance to him."

"Anyway," Jen continued, "when we first arrived here, Aaron told me about the laser machine he'd been working on. I told him about Karen and one thing led to another and she was recruited."

"To a good result," I might add, Aaron said. "Karen's got just what it takes to fire a laser."

"What's that?" Quinn asked.

"Nerves of steel."

Quinn grinned, "You've got that right."

He thought back to all they'd gone through to get to this spot at this moment in time. He'd started the journey by kidnapping Matt, but truth be told, he'd acted spontaneously with no real plan. It had been Karen who'd come up with the idea of getting them out of The City. Then Jen had joined them and together the four of them had made it across No Man's Land and into the mountains where Aaron had found them and brought them to Nedlaw where they were finally able to settle in their new home.

Then he had a thought. "Aaron, do you suppose we have to worry about repercussions because we shot down their drone?"

Aaron, who had been starring into the fire absent mindedly rubbing Jen's shoulder turned serious and said, "Yeah probably."

Quinn frowned. "Should we be worried?"

Aaron grinned, "Yeah, but not tonight. Tonight, we celebrate."

Matt woke up suddenly and said, "Celebrate? Celebrate what?" He hugged Joey. "I'm going to celebrate having Joey as my best friend."

The adults all laughed and nodded to each other. Quinn tossed another log on the fire and settled back with his family and two friends. He'd never been happier. He could stay here all night long as far as he was concerned. Forever. They had each other, and they had a new life, something better than they'd ever had before and for right now, that's all they needed. That's all that really mattered.

SOMETHING BETTER

Epilogue

LATER THAT NIGHT, under cover of darkness, a lone figure squeezed through a hole in the fence surrounding the Regional Food Storage Facility and adjusted his backpack. He turned toward the buildings and gave a silent salute. *So long suckers. I'm outta here.*

Buck Benson smiled. It felt good to be going. Really good. Rawlings was okay, but, standing by and doing nothing while Langer made him shoot that poor defenseless wild dog and then almost shoot that guy and those kids and the dog, it wasn't right. Even if he didn't kill those people, it was the principle of the thing that mattered. Buck grinned to himself. Principles. No one had ever accused him of having them before, but maybe he did.

Speaking of principles, or lack of them, rather, what about Langer? Man, the guy was a piece of work, a certified nutcase with no regard for human life at all. "Shoot to kill" was his motto, with no questions asked. The more Buck thought about it, the more it made him sick that innocent people could lose their lives for no other reason than they wanted to escape the tyranny of the World Order for a better life somewhere else.

Well count me in with them, Buck thought to himself as he turned away from the fence and started out across the desert some referred to as No Man's Land. Earlier that day, before the drone had blown up, he'd liked what he'd been seeing, especially the mountains. He liked the snow-covered peaks and the trees and the crystal-clear running water. He had a feeling he'd like the people in that little village, too. Thank goodness he hadn't had to kill any of them. He shivered a little at the thought. No, Buck was done with that kind of thing for good. For now, he was leaving The City behind and along with it his past and going forward to a new beginning.

He adjusted his pack and continued walking at a brisk pace. He was heading for the mountains. He didn't know what he'd find when he got there but he knew one thing, it had to be better than was he was leaving behind. Of that, there was no doubt in his mind. None at all.

SOMETHING BETTER

ABOUT THE AUTHOR

Jim lives in a small town twenty miles west of Minneapolis, Minnesota. His stories and poems have appeared in nearly three hundred online and print publications. His short story "Aliens" has been nominated by The Zodiac Press for the 2021 Pushcart Prize. His collection of short stories *Resilience* was published in early 2021 by Bridge House Publishing, and *Short Stuff*, a collection of his flash fiction and drabbles, will be published by Chapeltown Books in 2021. *Periodic Stories*, a collection of thirty-one stories based on the periodic table, was published by Impspired in early 2021. All of his stories can be found on his blog: www.theviewfromlonglake.wordpress.com.

www.ingramcontent.com/pod-product-compliance
Lightning Source LLC
Chambersburg PA
CBHW071255130626
46556CB00003B/1330